DROPSHIP MARINES

ERIC S. BROWN

SEVERED PRESS
HOBART TASMANIA

DROPSHIP MARINES

DROPSHIP MARINES

The *Vanguard* dropped out of Void space. Her automated systems were on full alert. Sensor arrays swept the Talia System in search of possible enemy vessels as her weapons powered up. Deep within her, other systems sprang to life, awakening her cargo from their long slumber. Power surged through the stasis pods within her hold.

Captain Allen Merrick's pod was the first to open. Its door lifted towards the ceiling of the hold as Merrick snapped awake, flinging himself from the pod. His senses were scrambled from the long sleep he had just been through. Flopping onto the hard metal floor of the hold, Merrick grunted from the unexpected pain of his shoulder meeting it. The impact and pain helped him shake free of the fog that still clouded his brain. All around him, other pods were beginning to open. He hurried towards his locker and began to don his flight uniform. Even as he did so, he addressed the *Vanguard*'s A.I.

"Status?" he barked.

"Good morning, Captain Merrick," the ship's A.I. answered him. "It is good to have you awake and functional again."

A part of Merrick's brain wondered if it really was morning or if the programmer who created the A.I. had simply designed it to greet him as he woke up from stasis in such a manner.

"Val..." he said to the A.I., an edge of anger and warning in his voice. "What's our status?"

"The *Vanguard* has reached the Talia system, Captain. All systems are optimal, and the awakening of the crew has commenced," Val told him in an overly happily simulation of a human voice.

"Any sign of—?" Merrick started, but Val interrupted him.

"All sensor sweeps are clear, Captain," Val informed him. "There are no signs of any other vessels within this system."

Merrick let out a sigh of relief, some of his frustration with the A.I. melting away at the news. Nonetheless, he wanted to get to the ship's bridge and confirm those readings for himself. No matter how advanced of an A.I. Val was, he didn't trust her to match the instincts of an experienced human spacer.

His XO, Phillips, came staggering towards the locker next to his own.

"Good to see you, Captain," Phillips told him weakly. "I trust all is well?"

Merrick nodded at the XO. "According to Val, everything's just as it should be. I'm on my way to the bridge now to confirm that."

"Yes, sir." Phillips tried to smile but honestly looked as if he were about to vomit on the deck plating of the hold's floor. "I'll be right behind you, sir."

Merrick ignored the rest of the ship's crew and the soldiers she carried who were beginning to stumble about the hold, heading for the bridge. He stepped into the nearest lift and grabbed hold of one of its hand braces to steady himself as it shot upwards through the ship. As he became more sure of his footing and ability to control the muscles of his body again, he released the handgrip and rubbed at his bruised shoulder. He wondered what he had to have been dreaming about that had made him launch himself out of his suspension chamber as he had. For the life of him, he couldn't remember. Merrick supposed it didn't matter. The *Vanguard*'s long journey was over and the real work was about to begin.

Merrick stepped from the lift onto the bridge of the *Vanguard*. He made his way across it to take his seat in the captain's chair. His fingers slid into the grooves on the end of chair's arms. Merrick felt the sharp crackle of the ship's energy flowing through him as his mind reached out to touch the systems of the *Vanguard*. He started re-running the scans that the ship's A.I., Val, had ran before awakening him. He double-checked the data from the scans, confirming that the *Vanguard* was not only where she should be, but also that the ship was alone in the Talia System.

The system only contained one Earth-like planet, and every study done by the Earth Gov. before the *Vanguard* had launched reported the planet to be empty of anything that could be a threat to the ship. Merrick was the sort who liked to be sure though. Too many lives rested in his hands for him not to be. Now, with the *Vanguard* less than two hours away from reaching orbit around Talia II, his own scans of the planet detected abundant life, both on and below the surface, but nothing even remotely technological in nature. No cities, no power sources, nothing that would give any indication of civilization upon the world. A sigh of relief escaped him as he removed his fingers from the grooves where they rested and disengaged from the ship's systems.

Not every ship in the Earth fleet had a tele-mechanic for its captain; in fact, such a thing was an extreme rarity, but then the

Vanguard wasn't just any ship. She was humanity's best hope for survival. The human race had expanded throughout the Sol System, but in order to survive, it had to keep expanding, reaching ever outward for new resources and new worlds to colonize much as the ancient Roman Empire had needed to expand in order to survive.

Captain Merrick wasn't the only psi-officer aboard the *Vanguard* either. He was merely one of seven. Earth Gov. had spared no expense in equipping the ship with the most advanced tech available but also in equipping her with the best of the best psionically as well. At the end of the 21st century, psionic abilities had gone from being the stuff of science fiction and fantasy to hard reality as the human race continued to evolve. Some believed that those with psionic abilities had evolved naturally as part of the course of human evolution. Others believed that the long-term exposure to the ambient radiation of space and the Void drive tech that allowed humanity to move freely among the stars had brought about the birth of psionic gifts. Merrick supposed it didn't matter how the first people with such gifts came about. They were here now, and he was one of them.

One out of every few thousand humans was born with a psionic gift. For some, those gifts were buried so deep within them that they were never discovered unless some kind of trauma brought their gift to the surface. Others were born with gifts so powerful that began to manifest on their own during one's teenage years. That had been how it happened with him. One day, everything was normal, and the next, he could "hear" all the machines and computers around him, feel them even. It had taken him months to learn how to control his gift enough to function properly in society again and longer still to master his gift to the point that he controlled it today. He didn't need the link provided by his captain's chair to interface with the *Vanguard* and her systems. The link only served to enhance his gift, fine-tuning it to a razor's edge, as he interacted with the ship.

Most tele-mechanics either became engineers or part of the Army's mechanized infantry, but Merrick had always dreamed of becoming a ship's captain like his father had been before him. The *Vanguard* and her mission had given him that chance. As advanced, well-armed, and well-crewed as she was, the powers that be knew the *Vanguard* would be cut off and alone for over six months during her flight through Void space to the Talia System and for another three months until the colony ships in route behind her caught up to her. Assigning a tele-mechanic as her captain just made sense. If anything went wrong with the ship, such a captain would sense it at once and be able to take whatever steps were needed to deal with the problem that had arisen.

The lift doors opened behind him, and Merrick turned to see his bridge crew reporting to take their stations with his XO Phillips leading them. His bridge crew took their stations.

"All clear, Captain?" Mr. Phillips asked.

Merrick nodded with a wry grin. "All clear."

"Val, all systems to manual," Merrick ordered the A.I. and then turned his attention to Lieutenant Patrick, his helmsman. "Confirm course for Talia II. Ahead three-quarters speed."

"Yes, sir," Patrick answered.

****

In the *Vanguard*'s hangar bay, Colonel Anna Stone was busy overseeing the preparations for planet fall. She and her marines would be the first humans to ever set foot on Talia II. Her men were working hard at loading the four dropships that would disembark from the *Vanguard* and carry them to the planet's surface once it established orbit around the unexplored world. Two of the dropships were devoted entirely to being personnel carriers. Another was to carry the supplies for her unit's extended stay on the planet. The largest of the four dropships carried the two APCs she planned on using to increase the amount of ground around the drop zone that her men could recon.

Stone noticed Sergeant Darcy and called to him. He came running over to her. Despite being fairly fresh from a prolonged stasis sleep, he stunk of sweat. It spoke volumes about how seriously the man took his job. He had been hands on, beside those under his command, loading the ships like an overly zealous new recruit.

"Colonel," he said, wiping sweat from his brow with the back of his hand so it wouldn't drip into his eyes.

"Don't skimp on the ammo, Darcy," Stone told him. "Cut back on some of the other gear if you have to, but make sure we have plenty of firepower available if we need it."

"Are we expecting trouble, ma'am?" Darcy asked.

"Quite honestly, Darcy, I have no idea what to expect down there," she admitted. "I'd rather be prepared than not."

"Makes sense," he grunted. "I'll see to it."

Darcy darted away from her barking new orders at a trio of soldiers near Dropship 2.

Stone jumped as a sudden voice from behind startled her as Leo said, "I don't foresee any trouble, ma'am."

Stone whirled on him. "What have I told you about sneaking up on me like that?" she growled. "One day, you may just find yourself with a bullet in your skull for it."

Leo chuckled. "I'd see it coming, ma'am."

"Your vision isn't that perfect, Leo," she reminded him.

Lieutenant Leo Barnes was her unit's precog. He was a portly man for a soldier and looked nothing like one would expect a member of the Colonial Marine Corps to be. There was always a cheerful smile on his lips, and his curly red hair only added to his boyish looks. His deep blue eyes were sharp though and betrayed the keen intelligence residing behind them.

"I rate Class B on the psi scale, ma'am," Leo laughed. "My ratio of accurately received visions of the future is well over eighty percent."

That was indeed impressive for a modern precog, Stone knew, but even so, that left an odd, close to twenty percent chance of error when Leo saw the things that were to come. His presence though was merely to advise her. Regardless of what his visions foretold, it was she who had the ultimate authority over their unit and how it proceeded both in combat and otherwise.

"I'm well aware of your gift, Lieutenant," Stone said. "I'm relieved to hear that you think we're in for a smooth op. when we land on Talia II, but you know I like to be cautious."

"No offense taken, ma'am." Leo smiled. "It's your job to get us through whatever comes at us and get us home. If you weren't overly cautious, I'd be concerned."

"Thank you, Leo." Stone placed a hand on the precog's shoulder. "Let me know if anything changes with the future you're seeing for us now."

"Always, ma'am," Leo assured her. "I want to keep breathing just as much as you do."

She saw Leo's lips curl up in an expression of disgust. Stone took her eyes off of him, following his gaze with her own. A rail-thin man dressed in black was walking towards them. The features of his face were as slick as his clothes were midnight black. His skin was stark pale and a pair of shaded goggles covered his eyes beneath the thick brown hair that topped his head. A pair of custom-made handguns with emerald butts were holstered on his hips. Stone couldn't help but wonder if he ever took the things off.

"Brasiliat," Leo said coldly, giving the man a slight nod of his head in greeting.

"Relax, Leo, I ain't got no business with you," Brasiliat answered just as coldly.

"To what do I owe the honor of this visit?" Stone asked. Brasiliat was her unit's advance scout and was even more of a loner than most scouts tended to be. Stone found it impossible to believe the man had ever passed the psych tests to be allowed into the military. She often wondered if the powers that be knew he had really failed them and didn't care. The man was deadly as they came even without his gift. In all her years, rising up to the rank of colonel, she had never met anyone else like Brasiliat. He carried an aura of death about him that even that even someone like herself, without a gift, could sense and feel. As scary as he was without his gift, seeing him use it in combat was the stuff of nightmares. His gift was violent in nature, but Brasiliat had learned to use it to enhance his natural born non-psi talent for dealing out death to any enemies she pointed him towards.

"This planet we're dropping onto…" Brasiliat started and paused uncharacteristically, as if he were searching for the right words to use, "…it's not right, Captain."

Stone frowned. "It's not right? If you have a concern about this mission, you're going to have to put in better words than that, soldier."

Brasiliat chuckled at the word soldier being used to describe him. "It feels wrong somehow," Brasiliat told her. "I don't know how to put it any better. Its *paths* are all messed up."

Paths was the word psycho-porters like Brasiliat used to describe whatever channels of unreality that they slid through from one point to another.

"You can sense that from out here?" Stone challenged him. "We haven't reached orbit around the planet yet."

"Aye, but we're close enough, ma'am," Brasiliat said. "Sure, I can't make a leap there yet, but whatever is wrong with that place extends into this star system, at least somewhat like a corruption that's filled up the planet and has overflowed. I can feel its taint reaching even into the corridors of this ship."

"You're wrong," Leo sneered at Brasiliat. "There's nothing wrong aboard this ship or on that planet either. I can't see anything ahead of us that would be troubling."

"You might want to stop and consider that whatever I am feeling may be affecting your gift too," Brasiliat pointed out. "You've been wrong before. We all know it, and more than a few have paid the price for it."

Leo's cheeks flushed with anger, but before he could speak, Stone placed a hand on his chest, stopping him.

"That'll be enough, Brasiliat," she warned. "No precog is perfect. We all make mistakes. The good Lord knows I do."

Her intervention appeared to calm Leo. Brasiliat's concern about the planet of Talia II worried her, however. It wasn't like the man to ever show any sort of worry, and here he was, coming to her no less, because he was that troubled.

"Will this…whatever…you're sensing in the paths," how she hated that name, "cause you any issues in using your gift?" she asked.

Brasiliat shook his head. "Shouldn't, but it makes sliding through the paths feel sort of like looking in a mirror."

"I can understand how that would be upsetting to you," Leo commented gruffly.

"Leo," Stone cautioned the precog then turned her attention back to her scout. "Captain Merrick and I can't scrap this op. because of a bad feeling from someone who doesn't have the gift of precognition and likely not even then Brasiliat. You know that. I am grateful for you coming to me with this though. If whatever you're feeling gets worse or changes, please let me know."

"Yes, Captain," Brasiliat answered. "Just thought you should know is all."

As Brasiliat walked away, Leo leaned closer to her and whispered, "Could that man be any more creepy?"

Stone ignored him. "Back to work, Leo. I know loading dropships isn't your thing, but you're here, and we can use all the hands we can get."

Leo looked like he wanted to protest being reduced to such manual labor but decided against it. He hurried to join those around the closest dropship to join up with them and see what he could do to help.

****

After the dropships were loaded, there was still an hour or so left until the *Vanguard* entered orbit around Talia II. Sergeant Darcy dismissed his men for them to get some much-needed rest. He stayed behind with the dropships though. He knew Sergeant Lesniak would have stayed behind too. Lesniak always enjoyed a good smoke before the unit made a drop, and it was just easier to do it alone in the hangar bay than anywhere else. Not that anyone in their right mind short of Colonel Stone or that whacked-out Brasiliat fellow would call Lesniak on it. Technically, it was against regs to smoke aboard ship, but exceptions were made, and the regs. were sometimes overlooked on voyages as long as the one to Talia II had been, even if you weren't the hulking, intimidating giant that Lesniak was.

Sergeant Lesniak stood a towering seven feet tall. Every inch of his body seemed to be made of hardened and toned muscle. He wore the scars of combat on his face and hands. The flesh of his hands was reddened and jagged from burns obtained in a battle long ago. His face was pockmarked with the scars left over from shrapnel that had torn and ripped away his skin. Darcy knew Lesniak could have requested the docs to fix him up right without a trace of his injuries, but the big man kept the scars as a reminder to "not get cocky" or so he said.

Darcy found Lesniak, just as he thought he would, in one of the hangar's far corners, leaning against the wall there and puffing on a fat cigar.

Lesniak smiled as he saw him coming. "Darcy!" he bellowed. "Just can't stay away, can you?"

"Your fault, you big barbarian," Darcy laughed, as Lesniak produced a second cigar, offering it to him along with his lighter. "You're the one who got me hooked on these things."

"They're good for you." Lesniak grinned.

"I doubt that," Darcy shot back. "More like cancer causing."

Laughter rumbled out of Lesniak like thunder. "But good for the soul all the same."

"You could have a point there," Darcy admitted as he lit up and leaned against the hangar wall next to Lesniak.

Darcy took a long drag from his cigar and breathed out the smoke. "You nervous?"

Lesniak shook his head. "What's to be nervous about? The entire human race is depending on us. No pressure there."

"Talia II is important," Darcy agreed, "but the human race won't end if things go wrong down there."

"Maybe not." Lesniak shrugged. "But it would sure be a good start towards an end. Without the planet to expand to, just think about what would happen back home."

"Some fighting maybe but nothing different than what we've seen before," Darcy argued. "I mean this op. is the biggest and most costly one going on right now, but it's far from the only one."

Lesniak had been fiddling with the lighter Darcy had given back to him. He slid the hand that held it forward, palm open with the lighter lying on it. The lighter floated up from his palm to hover above it as Lesniak changed the subject.

"You ever think about leaving the service, Darcy?" Lesniak asked as the lighter spun slowly in the air.

The question, coming from Lesniak, stunned him. He didn't know how to respond. He watched the spinning lighter above the big man's palm. Lesniak was one of seven psionically gifted members of those who had been assigned to the Talia II operation. The big man's gift had many uses but especially lethal ones. Lesniak was a very powerful telekinetic. The strength of his mind served to enhance the strength of his hulking and muscled body. Darcy had seen the big man kill enemy troops with nothing more than a glance and a thought. During the Rigel Rebellion, Darcy had even seen Lesniak go toe to toe with a tank and stand his ground. Lesniak had already been a hardened veteran and the survivor of dozens of drops when he himself had joined up. Lesniak had been something of a mentor to him. Darcy owed the big man more than he could ever repay. To hear Lesniak ask such a question was unthinkable to him.

"I do, Darcy," Lesniak confessed. "All the time these days. I've done my bit for Earth Gov. and split enough blood."

"You've been in the service, what, twelve years?" Darcy asked, still not believing what he was hearing from Lesniak but trying to hold it together for the big man's sake.

Lesniak nodded.

"That's a long time for anyone, Lesniak. I can't say that I blame you for feeling the way you do but man, come on, what would you do if you went back to being just a civilian? Could you even make that sort of change in your lifestyle now?" Darcy knew that Lesniak couldn't. The military was a part of him, sunk into him so deep that Lesniak would surely snap living any kind of life outside of it.

"Merc companies like the Hell's Banshees are always hiring," Lesniak said.

"Yeah, and that would change things for you how?" Darcy frowned. "From what I have heard about units like that, you would have more blood on your hands for sure, and not all of it justifiable."

Lesniak snatched the floating lighter from the air and flung his nearly finished cigar to the hangar floor, grinding it out with one of his heavy combat boots.

"I didn't say I had an answer, Darcy, just that I want out," Lesniak growled. "I have had my fill and I'm done after this op."

Darcy kept silent as he watched Lesniak walk away, leaving him alone in the hangar. He hated himself for not being able to be there better for his longtime friend, but what could he really do? If Lesniak wanted out, there would be no stopping him. The man was a juggernaut when it came to his force of will and determination. Darcy took another drag from his cigar, and this time let the smoke fill up his lungs entirely, savoring its feel and flavor, but even so, it didn't help to take the edge off of his emotions. Looking down at the cold metal of the hangar floor, he realized that what was feeling for Lesniak was more than just fear for the big man's future. It was pity and perhaps a trace of fear for what lay ahead in his personal future as well.

****

Captain Merrick sat in his command chair watching the image of Talia II on the bridge's forward view screen as the *Vanguard* entered orbit around the planet. Merrick reached out with his mind, running another scan of the planet through the ship's sensor array himself. Talia II was teeming with life, but above and below its surface.

The lift doors behind him opened and Specialist Rita Noel walked onto the bridge. Merrick had sent for her because he wanted to be as sure as he could about what he was sending Colonel Stone and her marines into.

Merrick skipped the pleasantries and got straight to business. "Rita, I need you to scan the planet…your way."

"Something wrong, Captain?" Rita asked.

Merrick shook his head. "Nothing as far as the *Vanguard*'s sensors can pick up. Everything checks out just like it should. There is abundant plant and animal life, an Earth-like atmosphere to the point of being almost identical, no signs of power sources or any tech for that matter."

"But…" Rita grinned.

Merrick shrugged.

"You know I can't accurately read an entire planet," Rita reminded him.

"Just open your mind to it and see if anything pushes back or tried to get into yours," Merrick urged and said more gently, "I am aware of the risk to you, Rita. If I truly believed there was anything that dangerous down there, I wouldn't ask. I need to know though before Colonel Stone and her troops are deployed on the surface. If they're walking into something…" Merrick paused.

"The good of the many versus the good of the one," Rita said, "I get it. Why not just ask Barnes? If something bad is going to happen, he would know, wouldn't he?"

"Barnes is good, Rita." Merrick sighed. "You're better."

Rita laughed. "Flattery, huh? I didn't know you had it in you."

"Not flattery, simple fact," Merrick assured her. "Precogs get glimpses of what could be. A telepath's take on things are more concrete."

"Fine," Rita agreed. "I'll do it."

Merrick watched as she closed her eyes. Her body seemed to relax as if she was letting down her guard, and she was. For any telepath, opening one's mind in such a fashion came with risks. Rita stood there for a few seconds then suddenly opened her eyes with a confused look on her face.

"What?" Merrick asked. "What is it?"

Rita met his eyes as she said, "I...I don't know. There's something strange. I'm not sure how to put it into words."

"Try," Merrick ordered her.

"Well, nothing pushed back against me," Rita said. "In fact, I couldn't sense anything in the order of higher intelligence but...I did sense something else. Holes might be a good way to describe them. Like individual spots or areas where I couldn't sense anything at all."

Merrick cocked his head to the side as he thought about what she had said. "You mean like something or somethings that are trying to shield their thoughts against you?"

Rita shook her head. "No. Not exactly. I didn't feel any shields resisting me, if that's what you mean. Just sort of areas of distortion for lack of a better term. They could very well be a natural product of the planet."

"I see," Merrick lied, though he really didn't. "But your take is that there are no higher lifeforms down there?"

"Not that I could tell," Rita confirmed. "Not from up here, at any rate."

"I know you're not part of Colonel Stone's..." Merrick started.

"But you want me to go down with them anyway," Rita beat him to the punch.

"Yes, I do, that is if you're willing to," Merrick said. "I won't order you."

"Sure." Rita rubbed at her temples. Lowering her mental shields hadn't been an easy thing for her given that she had to actively ignore the thoughts of the bridge crew and focus intently on the planet so as not to read anything personal from them. Even so, a few random thoughts and feelings of the bridge crew had been impossible to block out being so open. Captain Merrick was nervous, more than he should be. The helmsman was having a rather male fantasy about the comm. officer who was lost in her own thoughts about a date she had when she rotated off duty. The weapons officer was daydreaming about a vast battle in which he was the hero. It was all more than she had wanted or needed to know about any of them. Telepathy was very much a double-edged sword to her. From the time her gift had emerged, Rita had strived just as hard to fine-tune her mental shields as she had with all the other aspects of her gift combined. Knowing what others were thinking was nowhere near as fun as it sounded. More often than not, their thoughts reminded her of just how flawed humanity as a race was.

"Good." Merrick smiled. "Grab whatever you think you'll need and gear up. I'll have Stone and her bunch wait for you."

"Yes, sir," Rita answered and disappeared back into the lift.

Merrick watched her go and hoped he was making the right call. Having a telepath on the planet's surface with Stone's group had a lot of advantages. If something went wrong with the comms., Rita would be able to let them know what was going on, and he hoped she would act as a secondary warning system to Barnes and his visions of the future. Between the two of them, if there was anything dangerous at hand or coming, Colonel Stone should have plenty of warning to kick in its teeth or get the Hades out its way.

****

Ensign Mayhart screamed in agony, thrashing about on the table. His right hand was attached to his wrist by only bits of sinew and a jagged piece of stubborn bone that had refused to break completely when the loader had malfunctioned and dropped onto it.

"Hold him, blast it!" Dr. Joseph Lumley shouted at the two crewmen who had brought the ensign in. Their faces were pale and their uniforms were slicked with Mayhart's blood as they struggled to keep the ensign on the table.

Joseph had his sleeves rolled up as he entered the battle to get Mayhart under control himself. He needed the ensign still if he was going to do his work. Mayhart was in shock. There was no question about that. His eyes were wide as he fought against those trying to hold him. Joseph knew he could have Mayhart sedated but really there was no need for it. If he could just get his hands on Joseph's mangled wrist, the whole mess would be over in less than a minute.

Finally, Joseph got a good grasp on Mayhart. He clutched the remains of the ensign's wrist with both his hands. "Stop moving, man, and let me do my job!" he shouted at Mayhart.

Joseph ignored the ensign's thrashing and wailing and centered himself, focusing his thoughts. Psychic tendrils reached out from his mind to probe Mayhart's injury. Joseph took a breath and then let his own bio-energy flow into Mayhart. Flesh and bone grew beneath his touch. Joseph gave a final push with his mind, grunting from the effort, and then it was all over. Ensign Mayhart stopped struggling, his pain gone, as he stared as his wrist. It was intact once more with no sign that it had ever been nearly severed from his arm.

"See, kid, that wasn't so bad now, was it?" Joseph laughed.

"T-T-Thank you, Doctor," Ensign Mayhart croaked at him.

"You're good as new, young man. Now get out of my medical bay and back to work." Joseph smiled, though his tone remained rough enough to prompt the ensign into motion.

Ensign Mayhart eased himself from the table, stumbling to his feet.

"You'll feel a little weak for a few minutes," Joseph told him, "but it'll pass quickly."

The other two crewmen who had brought Ensign Mayhart him helped him towards the door.

"And blast it, be careful out there," Joseph called after them. "I don't want to see you back here for a good while!"

The med-bay's door closed behind them as the trio left.

Joseph collapsed into a chair next to the table that Ensign Mayhart had been on.

"You handled that well," Melina chuckled, "if not at all by the book."

Joseph was weak too. He always was after he healed someone. The greater the injury, the greater the strain on his system. He looked at Melina where she stood over him and said, "Sometimes speed is more important than procedures."

Melina frowned. "The auto-doc could have healed him just as well as you did."

"Yeah," Joseph admitted, "but we've got a lot of prep work to do to get ready in case everything goes pear-shaped when those ground pounders hit the surface of Talia II. I didn't want Tweedle Dumb and his buddies hanging around in our way while the auto-doc took hours to do what I did in seconds."

"That's funny, Dr. Lumley, because it looks to me like you're going to need a good bit of rest yourself now before we can get back to work." Melina smirked.

"I'm fine and you know it," Joseph growled and got to his feet. The room swam around him and he plopped back into the chair. "Okay, maybe just a little rest."

"Shall I finish the rest of the preparations then?" Melina asked, smug and full of herself in Joseph's opinion. He hated it when she was right. He was the blasted doctor and she was just a nurse. Right or not, there was no reason to rub it in.

"Go ahead and get back to it," Joseph ordered her. "I'll join you in a bit."

"Because I oh-so-love having all the work around here dumped on me again," she teased as she left him where he sat in the chair next to the table.

Joseph wondered why he kept the woman around. It was well within his power to have her booted from his med-bay and a new nurse brought in to take her place. He knew that was just his grumpiness talking, but it felt good to think he had that kind of power. In truth, Melina was the best nurse he had ever worked with. Her mind was like a steel trap when it came to the administrative parts of running the med-bay. Not a day went by when he didn't flat-out rely on her to make sure everything was as it should be and he stayed on track.

He could feel his strength seeping back into him. Joseph got up from his chair and walked over to his workstation. "Val," he said to the ship's A.I., "display image of Talia II."

"Yes, Dr. Lumley," Val answered, and a 3D-image of the planet appeared hovering over his desk.

Joseph stared at the image. Even from space, there was no mistaking how filled with life the planet was. The blues and greens of its color from orbit were breathtakingly beautiful. He wished he was accompanying Colonel Stone and her men to the world's surface, but as chief medical officer of the *Vanguard*, he was trapped aboard ship unless something went terribly wrong down there for the colonel and those who were accompanying her. Joseph had joined the Fleet to see new worlds, but for the most part, he only ever saw them from orbit. He hoped though that this time, given the nature of the op., that once a basecamp was established and secured, he could convince Captain Merrick to let him go down to the planet's surface. He wasn't an eco-path who could tap into the world itself or even a botanist or zoologist. His skills and psychic abilities were limited to the practical doctrine of healing and healing alone. Nonetheless, he dreamed of being able to explore worlds like Talia II and walk upon them.

Melina's voice tore him from his thoughts, "Hey, when you stop daydreaming, I could use a hand over here!"

Joseph sighed, shutting off the image of the planet, and mockingly shouted, "Yes, dear, I'm on my way!"

****

The dropships would be disembarking from the *Vanguard* within the next hour. Brasiliat knew the time had come. He was Colonel Stone's advance scout in situations like this one. Alone in his quarters and fully geared up, Brasiliat cleared his mind to focus on the planet below. He synced with it as his body vanished from the *Vanguard*, slipping into the folded pathways he traveled through. When he opened his eyes, he was sitting Indian-style in grass damp from morning dew. The walls of his quarters were gone, replaced by the thick trees in what appeared to be a cross between a jungle and a temperate forest. Talia II's sun was beginning its ascent into the sky, its rays piercing the foliage of the trees. The sunlight washed over his skin, making him feel alive.

Brasiliat remained motionless for a moment, his eyes scanning the woods around him to make sure he was alone. When he saw that he was, he rose to his feet. An edge of sickness from his transport tainted the otherwise peaceful and beautiful scene. He knew it was from the corruption that oozed along the psycho-portive pathways of this world he had brought himself to. It was nothing more than a mild annoyance, but it was enough to put him in a foul mood as he shook off its effect.

The woods around him were not just quiet but utterly silent. The silence was a touch unnerving but there were no signs of animal life, predator or otherwise. Brasiliat left his pistols in their holsters as he walked about the area he had transported into. Once he was completely sure he was alone, he blinked out of existence, reappearing a far distance from he where he had stood, staring into the clearing where he had been. Again, he checked his surroundings for signs of danger to find none. Blinking in and out of reality, his recon of the area expanded in a circular fashion, the pace of his blinks increasing as he went. When he had covered a five-mile radius, he sank to his hands and knees vomiting, long and hard, into the grass. Dry heaves shook him long after his stomach had emptied itself. The effect of the taint in the pathways of this world was apparently cumulative. There had been no means of knowing that until he had tested them out, however.

Wiping his mouth with the backside of his hand, he stood. Whatever the taint was, it was everywhere in the pathways and clung to his mind with each blink. Its effects seemed to wear off fairly quickly despite the rough patch on his knees. He felt fine now, though he could still sense the taint around him. His job was done for the moment, and he was thankful for it.

Steeling himself as best he could against the taint, he blinked into the clearing where he had first appeared once more at the center of the area he had scouted. Tapping the earpiece he wore to activate his comm., he reported in. "Brasiliat to the *Vanguard*. The LZ is clear. I repeat, the LZ is clear."

Brasiliat stood in the clearing, looking up into the sky. The others would be coming down to join him. There was no point in blinking back aboard the ship. He shrugged his backpack from his shoulders and took the landing beacon from it. Placing it in the center of the clearing for the dropships to hone in on, he activated it. All he could do now was to wait. On another world, he would have continued his scouting of its surface, but not on this one. Making himself sick once for the day was enough unless he was ordered to do again by the colonel when she arrived.

****

Sergeant Peter Lesniak looked around at the group of men and women, all in full combat and armed to the teeth, who shared the rear compartment of Dropship 2 with him. A few of the veterans like himself, appeared relaxed, but the bulk of the faces he saw wore expressions of nervousness. A couple of the newbies were a lot more than nervous. They seemed on the verge of panic as Dropship 2 made the transition from the *Vanguard*'s hangar into open space.

Lesniak yawned, longing for another cigar, though he knew he would settle for a cup of coffee. Neither was to be had though. He stretched inside the safety harness that ran over his chest in shape of giant X, its latch in its center. The drop would be over in a matter of minutes, and then the real work would start.

Lesniak and his counterpart, Sergeant Darcy, who was riding down on Dropship 1, had both been privy to Brasiliat's report on the planet's conditions. When the rear doors of Dropship 2 opened, he'd be charging into a very humid forest. Brasiliat had supposedly scouted a five-mile radius around the landing zone and found it clear of anything that could be a threat. Lesniak supposed he should be grateful that there wouldn't be bullets pinging against the dropship's hull and tearing into those under his command as they shambled out of its rear, but he just couldn't bring himself to do it. If there weren't bullets when they landed, something would surely come at them soon enough afterwards. That was the way of life in Colonial Marines. And sometimes, those threats that came at you later were the worst because you didn't always see them coming. They weren't there waiting for you, right in your face, as you charged out into them. Knowing your enemy and where to shoot when you touched down were things that newbies like Kurt and Daniel just didn't appreciate enough.

Dropship 2 entered Talia II's atmosphere, jarring those inside her about. Daniel, one of the unit's newbies, looked on the verge of vomiting. Chuck, another newbie, clutched the straps of his safety harness so tightly his knuckles were not only white but looked like they might split open from the amount of pressure he was applying on it. Lesniak stared across the rear compartment at them. Everyone could feel the dropship falling like a roller coaster that had reached the top of its track and was shooting downwards like a bullet. Sometimes, Lesniak wondered if the pilots of dropships like this just opted to have some fun on the way down with the ground pounders stuck in the ship's rear.

Finally, the dropship leveled out and the pilot's voice came over their comms. "Landing in two!"

Lesniak felt the dropship turning in the air as it picked its LZ. There was a final bump as it touched the ground. All the safety harness automatically disengaged. Lesniak was first to the rear door. He stood in front of it, blocking the path of the others.

"Okay, ladies and gentlemen," he called out. "We have ourselves a landing zone to secure. I want this done by the book. Do I make myself clear?"

A chorus of voices answered, "Yes, sir!"

The rear door opened, thudding onto the grass outside it, as Lesniak led the others out onto the surface of Talia II.

****

The marines from both dropships fanned out to secure the area around them. Colonel Stone emerged from Dropship I in their wake. She glanced over at Dropship III which had just touched down. Dropship III carried her unit's vehicles, and she was eager to see them deployed.

Brasiliat was waiting for her at the end of Dropship I's ramp as she walked down it.

"Colonel," he greeted her.

"Five miles, Brasiliat? You're slipping," she chided him.

Brasiliat grunted. "It's this planet, ma'am. Like I told you, the paths here are corrupted. Just doing a recon of five miles left me sick as a dog."

"Whatever is wrong with your pathways, Brasiliat," Barnes cut in as he joined them at the foot of the ramp, "it's likely just a natural occurrence of some sort. I wouldn't worry about it too much."

Stone saw the anger that flared in Brasiliat's eyes at Barnes' words.

"This ain't natural," Brasiliat growled.

Barnes gave the scout a dismissive wave. "Your job is done for now, Brasiliat. Why don't you get some rest?"

"With or without your gift, Brasiliat," Stone said, "You're the best scout I've met. I want to you head over to Sergeants Darcy and Lesniak. Assist them as you can."

"Yes, ma'am." Brasiliat nodded and darted away, clearly happy to be leaving Barnes behind him.

Stone turned to Barnes. "I wouldn't push him too hard if I were you, Barnes. You just might come to regret it."

It took a moment for Barnes to catch her meaning, but when the precog did, he swallowed hard and nodded. "Perhaps you have a point, ma'am."

Stone removed the hand-scanner she carried on her hip from her belt and fired it up. Holding it out, she swept the tree line with it. "Looks like we're really the only things here, other than the vegetation. Not that I am complaining, mind you."

The plan was for her unit to establish a safe and secured beachhead on Talia II and then recon to the nearby area of the planet where the ore that Earth Gov. was so interested in was supposedly located. Her hand-scanner confirmed that the ore was there exactly where it should be. Its location was a solid ten miles from the landing zone that was hastily being transformed into the unit's basecamp.

The next few hours were spent unloading the dropships. Once they were emptied, all three rose from the ground and headed back up to the *Vanguard* as per SOPs. Seeing them go made Stone uneasy. Their departure meant that she and her men were truly alone and that help was at least ten minutes away, even if the dropships were kept at alert status on the main ship in orbit. They wouldn't be, of course. There were no threats at hand to warrant such an action. That meant if something did happen, their response time would be closer to a half-hour response time, depending on the situation.

Brasiliat's continued talk of the corrupted pathways of the planet combined with Barnes' far-too confident predictions of things going smoothly put her on edge. Usually, if something looked too good to be true, that meant Hell would be coming shortly.

The two APCs from Dropship III were being brought online. Their sensors were far superior to the mere hand-scanner she had. Colonel Stone headed for the closest one. Its call sign was Alpha I.

The vehicle's driver had just emerged from inside it and gave a start as he saw her coming towards him.

"Colonel!" he exclaimed, snapping to attention.

Colonel Stone struggled to remember the man's name. She did her best to make sure she knew the names of everyone under her command, but this op. had been hastily assembled despite the amount of money and effort that had gone into it. There were several new soldiers to her unit that she didn't know by name and it irked her.

"What's your name, trooper?" she asked.

"Specialist Henry McGregor, ma'am," the young man answered.

"She ready?" Stone asked, gesturing at the APC.

"Online and ready to roll if need be, ma'am." McGregor smiled.

"Good work, McGregor," Stone told the specialist as she passed him, heading aboard the APC.

McGregor followed her. "Can I help you, ma'am?"

"Don't worry. This isn't an inspection, McGregor. I just want to use Alpha I's sensors," she assured him, seeing his concern.

Stone took a seat at the gunner station. The systems were online and up just like McGregor had said they were. If Captain Merrick were here, she thought, he could have ran the scan she wanted with only a thought. Gifted folks weren't all that rare these days, but they still seemed an oddity to Stone. Sometimes she wished she had a gift herself or at least wondered what having one must be like. What was it like to hear other people's thoughts or move through space like Brasiliat did? She had always heard that any such gift came with a downside to it. For Brasiliat, it made him an extreme loner. For Barnes, it made him one smug SOB. Captain Merrick's made him a social outcast in a sense too, like Brasiliat. Oh, Merrick could function just fine. It was just that he always came across as cold as the machines that he spoke with.

Putting her thoughts aside, Stone returned her focus to the task before her. She wanted a full scan of the area between the landing zone and the location of the ore. The APC's much more powerful sensors swept over the area, reporting back nothing different than her hand-scanner had. Stone sighed. It was still worth the effort to try.

"Everything okay, Colonel?" McGregor asked.

"Everything's just as it should be," she said, "and that's what worries me."

Meanwhile, Brasiliat had met up with Darcy and Lesniak. He had found the two of them standing outside of Alpha II, puffing on thick cigars that gave off a strong scent of vanilla.

"The colonel sent me over to assist you," Brasiliat told them. Technically, he outranked them, but Brasiliat detested any kind of authority, especially his own.

"Good to see you, Brasiliat." Darcy smiled at him.

Lesniak said nothing but offered him a cigar.

Brasiliat saw it and shook his head. "No thanks."

Lesniak grunted at him in disapproval and tucked the cigar back into a pouch on his belt. "Your loss."

"Not really anything for you to help with right now, sir," Darcy told him. "We're just waiting on the colonel to give the word to move out."

Darcy must have noticed the glance he shot towards Alpha II because he said, "Not in this! The two APCs need to stay at basecamp for the time being."

Brasiliat understood why too. The two APCs were the main firepower that the unit had its disposal.

"Colonel Stone is going to be sending a couple of squads out to confirm what you found on your recon and head on out to the location of the ore to set up another camp there," Darcy explained. "I'll be leading the one to the ore. The big man here will be taking the other. I'd love to have you along."

"Understood," Brasiliat answered.

Brasiliat saw Darcy's hand rise to the earpiece he wore under his helmet. "Yes, ma'am," Darcy answered then looked at him. "Looks like we're moving right now."

****

Sensor Tech Kathy Garrett stared at the screen of her station. There were disturbances showing up in Talia II's magnetic field. At first, she thought they were just glitches in the system. After running two full system-wide diagnostics though, everything with the ship's sensors checked out green. She asked Val to double check her and the A.I. did so, confirming that the system was full functionally and operating normally. Whatever the disturbances were, they were still there, appearing randomly for a fraction of a second only to disappear as if they had never existed. Garrett had no idea what the blips might be. Even the data she could get on them was confusing. Sometimes they registered as solids and others not. She was at a loss as to what to do next.

Garrett flinched as she heard Captain Merrick's voice behind her.

"I applaud your devotion and work ethic, Garrett, but not even you work this hard unless something's wrong," Merrick said. "What's going on?"

"To be honest, sir, I don't really know." Garrett shrugged as her cheeks flushed red with embarrassment.

"Try to explain it," Merrick urged her.

"Well, sir, there are some kinds of disturbances in Talia II's magnetic field. They appear at random points only to disappear in less than a second. There doesn't seem to be a pattern to them and both Val and I have checked out the system. Whatever they are, they aren't a glitch that's being caused by a malfunction."

Merrick's expression drew tight with concern. "These disturbances," he asked, "where are they?"

Garrett blinked, shocked that she hadn't thought to check their location, and knew she had failed in her job by not doing so. She watched for the next disturbance to pop up and locked onto it for the fleeting second it was on her screen. A muted gasp escaped her as she did so.

"They are all located within ten miles or so of the away group's landing zone where they are setting up base camp," she said.

"Interesting," Merrick whispered more to himself than her. "And from what you can tell, are these disturbances dangerous?"

"I don't think so, sir," Garrett said. "They aren't accompanied by EMPs and seem confined to a very small space when they appear. I doubt they would have any harmful effects to anyone who happened to be near one when it occurred."

"How small are they?" Merrick leaned to look over her shoulder at the screen in front of her.

"They vary, sir," Garrett told him. "Some are slightly larger than a man, others a touch smaller."

"And you have no idea what they could be?" Merrick pressed.

Garrett shook her head. "None, sir. According to Val, there's nothing in the ship's database that matches them. They appear to be unique to Talia II's magnetic field."

"I want you to keep at this, Garrett," Merrick ordered her. "Find out what those disturbances are. In the meantime, I'm going to let Colonel Stone know about your discovery. Perhaps her eyes on the ground can give a better idea of what's going on with them."

"Yes, sir," Garrett answered, redoubling her efforts to find an answer to the strangeness of the disturbances and their origin.

****

Lesniak's squad consisted of the two newbies, Daniel and Chuck, as well two veteran troopers, Ford and Jenkins. The four of them set out at the same time as Darcy's squad did. The two squads quickly parted ways though; Darcy's heading northward while Lesniak led his men south.

The big sergeant took point himself with Ford bringing up the squad's rear. Despite the peaceful seeming nature of the planet, all of them carried their weapons at the ready. Everyone but Lesniak carried standard issue rifles. He carried a custom-made shotgun in place of one. Its three barrels formed a rough triangle at the end of the weapon and had enough firepower to them to put even a shielded telekinetic on their arse. Knockdown power mattered a lot to Lesniak. That was why he opted for the shotgun.

It was the afternoon sun that was terrible despite the cover of the trees. The same cover that shielded them from the worst of its rays also acted to trap the heat down among the trees with them. Lesniak wiped sweat from his eyes. He and his squad had been walking for over an hour now at a brisk pace. He removed his hand-scanner from his belt and activated it, sweeping up in the direction they were moving in to make sure they were still on track. The scanner confirmed that they were. The ore deposit was roughly another five miles ahead of their current position. The scanner beeped at him as it registered…something. Whatever it was, it blinked in and out of existence too fast for Lesniak to get a real reading of it. It had been close though. Too close from him to feel comfortable about. He stopped walking as he raised a hand, gesturing for those behind him to do the same.

"Hey, Ford!" Lesniak called to his man on point. "Hold up!"

Jenkins came running up from the squad's rear to join him at the front. "What is it, Sarge?"

"Something was moving over on our right flank," Lesniak explained. "Anyone get a look at what it was?"

The newbies, Chuck and Daniel, shook their heads.

"I didn't see anything either," Jenkins added.

"What's the plan?" Ford asked.

Lesniak stared at the screen of his hand-scanner. "Whatever it was, it may be gone already."

"Yeah, and it might not." Ford had his rifle aimed towards the squad's right flank.

"This thing isn't registering it anymore," Lesniak told the others. "Of course, that don't mean squat. Sometimes these things are utterly useless."

Suddenly, without warning, the scanner beeped again. Something popped onto its screen to the squad's left only to vanish as quickly as it had appeared. Lesniak whirled to try to catch sight of whatever it was but was too late. All he saw were trees and shadows.

"Anybody get a look?" he asked.

"At what?" Ford grumbled. "I didn't see crap."

Daniel raised his hand like a kid in a classroom.

Lesniak shot him an angry glare. "What Daniel? You don't have to raise your freaking hand to talk out here!"

"I saw the trees move, Sarge," Daniel stammered.

"The trees?" Jenkins challenged the newbie. "Are you really saying you saw a bloody tree move?"

"No, sir!" Daniel snapped. "I'm saying I saw the lower limbs of one of them shift and sway a bit like something had just moved by them at high speed."

"That's better, Daniel." Lesniak smiled. "Tell it like it is. Doing so without hesitation might just keep us all alive out here sometime."

Lesniak heard Colonel Stone's voice calling to him through his comm. He tapped his earpiece and said, "I read you, ma'am. Go ahead."

There was some static, but her words still came through loud and clear.

"Sergeant Lesniak, be advised that the *Vanguard* has picked up some strange activity near your position. The ship's sensors can't get a good read on what's happening around you. Captain Merrick wants you to check it out but with extreme caution. Understood?"

"Yes, ma'am," Lesniak agreed. "Consider us on it. If there's something out here, we'll get eyes on it ASAP."

Lesniak ended the transmission, turning to his squad. "So it appears that really is something out here with us. We need to find out what it is ASAP."

"And, uh, how exactly are we going to do that, Sarge?" Ford challenged him. "I mean, we were standing right here as whatever it is passed by twice and couldn't get eyes on it."

"Let's assume whatever it is, it's still here. Everybody spread out, weapons hot, and eyes on the trees at all times. If you see anything unusual, don't be afraid to open fire on it. I'd rather us kill some native lifeform by accident if we have to than have whatever it is out there moving around take down on of us," Lesniak ordered.

The squad members spread out, forming a rough circle, with each of them at least ten feet from the others. The forest was just as silent as it had been since they had landed. Lesniak's comment about blowing away a native lifeform made it click home in his mind that they hadn't seen a single lifeform that wasn't a plant on this planet so far. Not a single one. A planet this rich in vegetation and atmosphere should have been teeming with some sort of small game at least, yet there was nothing. Lesniak didn't know what to make of that fact beyond that it really was beginning to creep him out.

Though he had ordered the squad to spread out, he made sure everyone remained in line of sight with the others. It was a hard thing to do given the density of the trees, but they had managed it. Lesniak held his hand-scanner in one hand and his shotgun ready in the other as he waited on whatever was out there to circle around them again.

****

Barnes climbed into the APC. Colonel Stone was sitting at its gunner station looking frustrated.

"Something wrong?" Barnes asked.

Stone shrugged. "The *Vanguard* has detected some strange disturbances in Talia II's magnetic field."

Barnes frowned. "Nothing that would be a danger to us, I trust."

"I couldn't get a clear answer out of Captain Merrick on that," Stone replied. "I'm not entirely sure he knows the answer to that one himself."

"The bulk of our gear and equipment is hardened against EMP," Barnes pointed out.

"I'm not worried about an EMP," Stone said. "What worries me is how these disturbances are acting."

"Acting?" Barnes almost laughed. "That makes it sound as if you believe they are alive."

"I've been monitoring the disturbances since the word about them came from the ship," Stone told the precog. "They seem to be only occurring near our basecamp and the two parties we sent out."

"And you believe the planet may be reacting to our presence?" Barnes questioned her.

"Maybe. I don't know. It's just too much of a coincidence, isn't it? I mean that these disturbances are so localized and focused on us." Stone turned her gaze back to the gunner station's screen as another blip appeared on it near the position of Sergeant Lesniak's squad and then vanished.

"Too bad no one thought to assign a Ferro-kinetic to this operation," Barnes complained.

Stone huffed at the precog. "It's impossible to think of everything. Besides, who could have foreseen us running into anything like this?"

Barnes flushed. "Is that an insult, ma'am?"

Stone realized who she was talking to. "No, Barnes. Don't take that personally. I'm not blaming you or the other precogs who worked on assembling the personnel for this mission. I'm just…frustrated, I guess. I don't like unknowns, Barnes. Unknowns can get you killed."

"No offense taken, ma'am," Barnes said, but Stone could see from how he shifted about on his feet that his words weren't entirely true.

"I think it's time we tried something else," Stone announced getting up from her seat at the gunner's station. "Captain Merrick added Noel to our unit right as we were disembarking from the *Vanguard*. Have you seen her since we landed?"

"Specialist Noel has been helping out with the final inventory of the supplies we brought with us," Barnes said.

"Go get her, Barnes, and bring her here to Alpha I," Stone ordered.

As Barnes left, Stone noticed that Specialist McGregor was still standing nearby, watching her.

"What is it, McGregor?" she asked, the lanky driver.

"Nothing, ma'am," he replied, looking sheepish.

"If you're worried I am going to bust you for the issues I am having with Alpha I's sensors, I'm not. Even the *Vanguard*'s sensor array couldn't determine what those disturbances are," she assured him.

"It's not that, ma'am," McGregor said. "It's just rare to see a C.O. so hands on."

Stone laughed. "You're new to my unit, aren't you, McGregor?" she asked, knowing full well that he was.

"Yes, ma'am. Just transferred in for this mission." McGregor nodded.

"You'll find that there a lot of things we do differently in my command, McGregor," Stone smiled.

McGregor returned her smile. "I am sure it will prove to be an interesting experience."

At that moment, Barnes re-entered Alpha I with Specialist Noel in tow.

Noel presented herself professionally. "You wanted to see me, Colonel?"

****

Chief Engineer Waters walked the length of the *Vanguard*'s engine room, giving it his daily inspection. All of his people were good at their jobs, so he didn't expect to find anything amiss. Nonetheless, it was his habit, and they had long grown accustomed to his ritual to the point that most of them didn't even notice him as he strolled by them.

The long trip to Talia II with the crew in stasis had left much maintenance to be caught up on. Waters figured it would take them a few days to catch up on it all. The *Vanguard's* main systems were fine despite the lack of attendance beyond the automated, built-in systems.

"Sir!" Ensign Boyes came running up to him. The unusual occurrence instantly snapped Waters into crisis mode. From the way Boyes was acting, the main reactor might be about to blow.

"What is it, Ensign?" Waters asked as Boyes reached him.

"Call from the bridge, sir!" Boyes nearly shouted at him. "Captain Merrick says there's a magnetic disturbance of some kind in the maintenance shafts!"

Waters' eyes bugged at the panting ensign who was trying to catch his breath. "That's impossible!" he snapped. "The sensors down here would have sounded an alarm if that were the case."

"That's what I told the captain, sir, but he was rather insistent. He wants it checked out ASAP."

Waters frowned, shoving the ensign ahead of him towards the closest entrance to the shafts that lined the engine room. "Did he say where?"

"Yes, sir!" Boyes thrust a hand-scanner at him. "This is the position of the disturbance."

Waters took the scanner and looked at its screen. The disturbance wasn't far from them at all. He picked up his speed, running for the entrance to the shafts.

"Chief!" Ensign Boyes yelled after him. "The captain said to be careful, sir! He's dispatching a security squad to accompany you into the shafts!"

Waters heard the ensign but opted to ignore him. The position of the magnetic disturbance was close to a primary junction of the *Vanguard*'s primary control systems. If an EMP went off that close to it, the whole ship could be in some serious trouble. He did wonder why in Hades the captain was sending a security detail, but there was no time to waste. Someone had to get in there and see what was going on.

As Waters flung open the entrance to the maintenance shaft, *something* was waiting for him. His mind didn't have time to even register the features of the thing before it threw itself at him. Waters screamed as claws tore at his flesh. Blood splattered the open door of the shaft and the floor of engineering as Waters toppled backwards to land hard on his butt. His scream was silenced by the fact that his tongue and lower jaw had been ripped from him. He sat there, in shock and unable to move, bleeding onto the floor as the creature from the shaft moved by him. It was little more than a blur as it streaked towards Ensign Boyes. Waters saw the young ensign turn to run, but the creature was on him before he could. The room was spinning around Waters as he fought to stay conscious and failed. The last thing he heard were the young ensign's terrified and pain-filled screams.

****

Corporal Will Whiteside burst into engineering with Higgins and Sharps behind him. All three of the security officers had their sidearms drawn and ready. Whiteside had tried reaching Chief Waters via his personal comm. but there was no response. The moment he entered engineering, he saw why. There were bodies everywhere. The walls and floor were slicked with blood. Corporal Whiteside had expected trouble, he always did, but nothing like what he had come running into. His feet slipped from underneath on the blood-slicked floor and he fell, crashing to his hands and knees. His weapon flew from his grasp and went bouncing away from him.

"Holy!" he heard Higgins yell. Corporal Whiteside slid around in the blood soaking the floor, smearing it into his uniform as he struggled to get to his feet. He barely saw the thing that darted passed him towards Higgins and Sharps. Whatever it was, it was big. At least the size of a man.

Higgins and Sharps opened fire. Their pistols barked as the creature roared in fury at them. Corporal Whiteside stared at the creature in utter horror. He could only see its backside, but the thing was covered in black hair from its head to its clawed feet. Large wings spread out beneath its arms and its ears were huge and pointed, much like an Earth bat's. Its arms and legs were thick with muscles that rippled under the hair covering its body as the thing moved.

Bullets hammered into the creature's body. Black blood spurted from where they punctured its body, but they didn't even slow it down. It plowed into Higgins and Sharps, knocking the two men from their feet. A swipe of its claws, so fast that Corporal Whiteside could barely see it, reduced Higgins' face to a mess of mangled flesh. Higgins was dead before his body hit the bloody floor. Sharps landed with a loud thud next to Higgins' corpse. Sharps was still in the fight though. From where he lay, he raised the barrel of his weapon up at the creature as it swept over him. He got off three more shots that drew blood before the creature's razor-like claws severed his raised hand at the wrist. It and Sharps' weapon went flying as the creature descended upon him.

Corporal Whiteside was on his feet now. With a start, he remembered that his pistol was gone. He had no weapon to engage the creature with as it flopped on top of Sharps and began to tear him to shreds. Corporal Whiteside spotted his pistol a few feet away and raced towards it, careful not to lose his footing again.

Snatching up the weapon, Corporal Whiteside spun around as the creature finished its grizzly work upon Sharps and rose to stand at its full height. It stood a good seven feet tall as the creature's red-smeared lips curled into a snarl. Corporal Whiteside took aim at the creature's head as it lunged towards him. His pistol bucked in his grasp as he squeezed its trigger in rapid succession. His first shot sent a geyser of black blood spraying into the air. The creature's head was jerked back from the shot's impact as his second round missed its target and slammed into the creature's right shoulder. His third left a trail of oozing black on the creature's cheek as it gazed the thing's flesh. Then the creature threw itself upwards, dodging his next two shots, sweeping along the ceiling, to drop onto him from above.

Corporal Whiteside tried to track the creature's movement with the barrel of his pistol and keep his aim on it, but the creature was just too fast. One of its hands lashed out in a downward swipe that shredded his nose and crushed his eyes inside their sockets.

A pain cry escaped his lips as Corporal Whiteside's world went red and then completely dark. He didn't see the creature's mouth as its jaws distended, but he felt its teeth as they sunk through the bone of his skull with the sickening, crunching sound of bone cracking and caving inward.

Corporal Whiteside's body twitched for several moments on the grisly floor of the *Vanguard*'s engineering section before it finally stopped and lay still.

****

"How many again?" Captain Merrick asked Sensor Tech Garrett as she hunched over her workstation, trying to keep up with the number of magnetic disturbances appearing on its screen.

"Dozens, sir," Garrett answered. "The magnetic disturbances are popping up all over the ship. There's at least one on every deck."

"Raise shields and go to General Quarters," Captain Merrick ordered.

The lights on the bridge dimmed, tinting red, as the *Vanguard* shifted into battle mode.

"Is there any word from engineering?" Captain Merrick asked, trying to keep his voice as professional as possible.

"None, sir," Garrett informed him. "I can't reach the chief or anyone else down there. Not even the security squad is answering their comms."

The bulk of the Colonial Marines that were assigned to the ship were already on the planet's surface. That left him with only a handful of troops and his own security personnel to deal with whatever happening. He simply didn't have enough manpower to dispatch a squad to the sight of all the disturbances.

"Send all the marines left aboard to engineering. Tell them to assume that we have been boarded by an unknown force and take appropriate action. I want two squads of our security staff on the bridge ASAP. Dispatch the rest to deal with the disturbances closest to the key areas of the ship," Captain Merrick barked at Garrett.

"And the other disturbances, sir?" Garrett asked.

"We don't have the manpower to deal with them all, Garrett, not with Colonel Stone and her people on the planet. Route engineering control to your sensor station. I want you to try to enclose any of these disturbances that aren't being attended to in internal shields if you can. If you can't, close off the emergency bulkheads around them."

"On it, sir!" Garrett snapped and went to work at carrying out his orders.

Captain Merrick left Garrett to her work and returned to his command chair as the door of the bridge's lift opened. Four armed security officers stepped onto the bridge.

"Take up positions around the door you just came through and don't let anything through it that I don't personally authorize," Captain Merrick told them.

"Linda," he called to his comm. officer, "get me Colonel Stone, open channel. She needs to be informed of what's happening up here."

A few seconds later, the surprised voice of Stone rang out over the bridge's comm.

"Captain?" she asked. "To what do I owe the honor of this call?"

"The magnetic disturbances we've been detecting planet-side have spread to the *Vanguard*. I believe that we are under some form of attack," Captain Merrick told her.

"Sweet heaven," Colonel Stone rasped. "How is that even possible?"

"I wish I knew," Captain Merrick sighed. "What I do know is that I have a situation unfolding up here that may render us unable to offer you any assistance should you run into trouble on the planet. I'll be back in touch when I know more."

"Understood, Captain," Stone answered before Captain Merrick ended the transmission.

"Captain!" Garrett shouted at him. "I've been able to run a sweep of engineering with the internal sensors. I was able to find a way around the interference that the magnetic disturbances are causing aboard ship."

Garrett's expression was grim and close to panic. Captain Merrick knew the news wasn't going to be good before he even asked, "And?"

"Everyone in engineering, including the initial security response squad, is dead, sir."

Silence fell over the bridge as the rest of its staff looked up from their work at Garrett's shocking announcement.

****

The seconds ticked by like eternities as Sergeant Lesniak and his men watched for any sign of movement among the trees. His hand-scanner had been quiet for a long while now. Lesniak was ready to call it and give up when the scanner finally beeped again, indicating another one of the magnetic disturbances nearby. Its beep was followed almost instantly by a scream of pure terror from Chuck.

The monster, there was no other name Lesniak could give the thing, appeared out of nowhere, like a psycho-porter making a jump. It stood on two human-like legs, naked from head to toe, though covered in a thick black hair or fur. There were wings folded up under its thick, muscled arms. Its eyes weren't eyes at all. The sockets that should have held them were nothing more than thick areas of grey flesh, as if the thing's ancestors might have had eyes but evolution had robbed the creature of them. It towered above Chuck, standing over seven feet tall. Chuck didn't have time to react before he was dead. One of the monster's hands shot outwards, raking the razor-like claws of its fingertips over Chuck's throat. There was an explosion of blood from the jagged and shredded flesh that the claws had left in their wake. Chuck's corpse dropped into the grass, blood still spraying from the remains of his throat.

"Take the thing out!" Lesniak yelled, already sweeping his shotgun around in the monster's direction. It boomed like thunder as he squeezed the trigger that fired all three of the weapon's barrels at once. The blast caught the monster dead on as it turned towards the sound of his voice. Its chest caved inward as the shotgun's heavy slugs reduced its ribs and flesh to little more than pulp. Even as the monster's body fell, streams of automatic fire from Daniel and Ford tore into it.

The monster's ravaged form lay motionless on in the grass next to Chuck's corpse.

"Is it dead?" Daniel asked.

"Frag well better be!" Ford shouted.

"Ford, check it out," Lesniak ordered as he pumped a trio of fresh shells into the chambers of his shotgun.

Ford crept cautiously towards where the monster rested in the grass. As he approached it, he kept his weapon trained on it. When he got close enough, he gave the monster's body a solid kick with one of his combat boots. There was no reaction. Ford shoved the barrel of his rifle up against the side of the monster's skull and pulled the trigger. The point-blank burst blew a hole clean through the monster's head, sending black blood, brain matter, and bone fragments flying. The monster's body twitched one time then lay still once more.

"If it wasn't dead before, it sure as frag is now," Ford called out.

Lesniak and Daniel moved to join Ford near the monster's body.

"What in the holy Hades is that thing?" Daniel muttered.

"Heck if I know," Ford growled, moving a hand to cover his mouth and nose. "It smells like a pile of—"

"It looks like a cross between a demon and a bat," Lesniak chimed in, interrupting Ford.

"And a man," Daniel added before he turned around, dropped to his hands and knees, and started vomiting into the grass.

"Its eyes are the creepiest part of it," Ford commented.

"What eyes?" Lesniak asked.

"That's my point." Ford grimaced.

A moment of silence ticked by.

"Frag me, Sarge," Ford said, "Do you think there are more of them?"

"Stop saying frag," Lesniak growled. "I need to get the colonel on the comm. and report this."

Lesniak had dropped his hand-scanner when the action started. It beeped again from it rested in the grass.

"Frag!" Ford shouted as another monster appeared, flying through the air on wide-spread wings to swoop onto Daniel. It picked up the newbie, dragging him up with it to throw him against a nearby tree.

Lesniak flinched as he heard the sickening sound of Daniel's bones breaking as the newbie struck the tree at what had to be close to fifty miles an hour. Daniel's twisted form bounced from the tree to go rolling away from it. His shotgun thundered as Lesniak took a shot at the monster, but it was already gone, vanished back into the nothingness from it had come. He saw Ford staring at him with wide eyes.

"Run!" Lesniak shouted, whirling about to charge into the trees in the direction of the unit's basecamp. His legs pumped beneath him as he pushed his body to its limits, pumping another load of rounds into the chambers of his shotgun as he did so. Ford was on his heels every step of the way. The two of them kept close, but making sure to stay out of each other's line of fire as best they could, considering that they had no idea which direction the monster would come at them.

Lesniak regretted abandoning his hand-scanner, but the second or less of warning it gave them wasn't really enough to make much of a difference. Still, even a fraction of second warning was better than none.

"Sarge!" Ford shouted at him. Lesniak heard Ford's warning just in time to skid to a halt as the monster that appeared in the tree to his right came leaping off one of its upper limbs at him. There was no time to bring his shotgun fully to bear, so instead he used it as a club, meeting the monster's snarling mouth with its butt. Razor-sharp teeth broke and shattered inside the monster's mouth as Lesniak's telekinesis kicked in on instinct, increasing the force of the blow he dealt the creature with the butt of his shotgun. Black blood splattered over him as he stepped to the side, avoiding the creature's stunned body as it plunged into the grass near him. Lesniak spun his shotgun around in his hands, taking aim at the monster where it lay on the ground. He fired all three of the weapon's barrels in one gigantic burst, but the monster was already gone. It had blinked away as if it had never been there to begin with. The blast from the shotgun struck the forest floor, sending chunks of grass and dirt upwards in a miniature explosion.

The creature, or another like it, appeared behind Ford. Lesniak had no time to shout a warning at Ford. He didn't need to though. The creature's shadow had fallen over Ford and it was all the warning the veteran, colonial marine needed. Ford threw himself from the monster's path, rolling across the grass, as its claws slashed through the empty air where he had stood only a moment before.

Lesniak grabbed the monster with his mind, holding onto it with all his mental strength.

He could feel the creature fighting him, its strength of will against his own, and in that moment, he knew the creature was trying to teleport away. As the two of them wrestled mentally, Ford hosed the monster, his rifle set to full auto. A stream of high-velocity rounds ripped into the monster. They cut a path of gore from its stomach to the top of its chest. The monster gave a shriek of pain as the bullets dug into its flesh. The shriek took Lesniak by surprise and caused him to lose his focus. His mental grip on the monster was broken. It blinked away, only to reappear a few feet from where it had been, staggering as blood poured from the jagged mess of the wounds Ford had inflicted upon it.

"Finish it!" Lesniak yelled at Ford who was already swinging his weapon around towards the monster's new position. It was clear the monster was hurting. Lesniak figured it had intended to move a lot further away from them than it had when it tried to teleport but no longer had the strength to do so.

Ford nailed the monster first. Rounds from his rifle tore into its side, drawing fresh blood, as Lesniak readied his shotgun. The monster managed to raise itself up to its full, seven-foot height and was about to leap at Ford as Lesniak's shotgun boomed. The trio of slugs from its barrels blew the monster's head apart in an explosion of black pus and bone fragments that soared through the air like shrapnel from a detonating grenade. Its headless body swayed back and forth before collapsing to the forest floor.

"We have to keep moving!" Ford shouted.

"Roger that!" Lesniak shouted back following after Ford had lunged into motion and was sprinting through the trees, ducking under low-lying limbs and bounding over the thick roots of older trees that poked up through the grass.

****

"You want me to do what exactly?" Noel asked.

Colonel Stone sighed as McGregor and Barnes watched the two of them.

"I want you to reach out and open your mind to one these magnetic disturbances that are popping up all over the planet and now aboard the ship in orbit too. I need to know if they are alive," Stone explained.

"Why would you think that they would be alive?" Noel asked.

Technically, Noel was part of Captain Merrick's crew and not a direct part of Stone's unit. Stone knew she had very little authority over the telepath. Nonetheless, she needed Noel to try not waste time with questioning her.

"Listen to me, Noel," Stone said. "These things don't seem to be as random as they appear. The fact that they are only occurring near where we are on this planet and have now spread to the *Vanguard* is very disturbing. Call it a hunch if you want, but I suspect they are a lot more than just some sort of natural phenomena. For all we know, they could be a coordinated means of recon. Something out there could be checking us out, finding our weak spots, before it makes its real move."

Noel nodded her understanding. "Point me at one of them then, I guess."

Stone gestured for Noel to come over Alpha I's gunner station with her. She sat Noel in the station's chair, leaning over her shoulder. "When you see a blip appear on that screen in front of you, reach out to its location."

One of the magnetic disturbances appeared almost instantly. Their frequency and density had greatly increased in the area where Sergeant Lesniak's squad should be by now. Stone watched Noel's lips tighten as the telepath strained to make contact with the disturbance. Noel's eyes shot wide as her mouth dropped open. She sat that way for maybe a second before she started to jerk about in the chair she sat in. Her body shook as if she was having a seizure, then the screaming started. Noel wailed in pure terror. Stone grabbed a hold of her shoulders, shaking her.

"Snap out of it, Noel!" Stone yelled. "Don't let whatever it is drag you in!"

Stone wasn't a telepath. She didn't have a psychic gift of her own. She had, however, worked with gifted men and women long enough to know that something bad, very bad, was happening to the telepath.

Noel continued to jerk about in the chair. Stone spun the chair around so that Noel was facing her and hauled her arm back. She slapped Noel across her cheek hard enough for the sound of the blow to echo inside the confined space of the APC.'s rear. Noel came awake like a drowning woman clawing her towards the surface to gasp for air.

"What the devil happened, Noel?" Stone barked at the telepath, but Barnes was suddenly at her side, pulling her away from Noel.

"Give her some space, ma'am," Barnes said. "She needs a moment to recover."

Stone resisted the urge to deck the precog, but then she saw the tears streaming from Noel's eyes and knew he was right.

"Sorry," she muttered to no one in particular.

"Don't worry about it, ma'am," McGregor told her. "If I were under the stress that you are, I would have done a lot worse."

Somehow, McGregor's words didn't bring her any comfort. Stone waited for Noel to become calm again and the telepath's sobbing to stop.

"You okay now?" Barnes asked Noel in a gentle voice.

"That was horrid," Noel stammered.

"What was it that you felt?" Stone pressed. "Are the disturbances alive?"

Noel shrugged. "That one isn't anymore. I linked with it as it died."

"Lesniak," Stone said aloud. "Given where that one popped up, I'd say he's the reason it's dead."

"A good bet to be sure," Barnes agreed.

"Did you get anything else? Do you know what we're up against?" Stone questioned Noel.

The telepath shrugged. "All I got was hunger, pain, and an anger so intense it burned in like a supernova in my mind. Whatever those disturbances are, they are alive; alive and really ticked off."

"That not good," McGregor commented.

"Then the *Vanguard* really is under attack," Barnes added.

"Looks like it," Stone agreed. "That means we are very likely on our own down here on the surface for the time being."

"I don't understand why I couldn't foresee this." Barnes frowned.

"Whatever it was that I linked with," Noel said, "it had a mind and a very powerful if completely alien one."

"Are you saying that whatever is out there is gifted?" Barnes asked.

"I wouldn't rule it out," Noel answered. "It was certainly intelligent and strong enough to be."

"This just keeps getting worse and worse." Stone shook her head. "Barnes, I want you to triple the security around the base camp's perimeter. McGregor, I want Alpha I and Alpha II ready to engage anything that gets too close the camp. We may need the extra firepower these APCs can bring to bear on whatever is out there. Noel, take whatever time you need to recover, but if you remember anything else you got from the link, let me know at once."

"Sounds like we're getting ready for war," Barnes said. "Are you sure we're in it that deep?"

"Whatever these creatures that are behind the disturbances we've been picking up may be, they've already had plenty of time to study us and may even already be in the process of making a hostile move aboard the ship in orbit. We need to be ready for them and geared up to blow them back to whatever Hell they crawled out of," Colonel Stone growled. "You all have your orders, so I suggest you get to it. I'll stay here with Noel and get on the horn with Lesniak and Darcy. Lesniak's squad has likely already been hit from what Noel has told us, but Darcy and his men likely have no idea what kind of danger they might be in. Someone needs to let them know."

****

Sergeant Darcy's squad had set out for the location of the ore that Earth Gov. so desperately wanted Talia II. The planet would also open more living space for the citizens of the Earth Republic to expand to as colonists flocked to the new world, hoping to improve the hand fate dealt them with a fresh start. Others would come to capitalize on the planet's resources and still others would come merely seeking the adventure that a life on a new world could offer them. But it was the ore that had been the reason for an initial military expedition sent ahead of the usual colony ship. Earth Gov. wanted the ore secured and in their own pocket before mere businessmen could claim a stake to it.

The sun was beginning to set in the sky, though Darcy and his squad were still two miles from the ore's location. Brasiliat was slowing them down. Every so often, the scout would stop to examine the forest and take in the lay of the land. Darcy knew that Brasiliat could travel through the pathways of Talia II without needing to know its landscape first hand, but he knew too that having an image in one's mind when blinking from point A to point B certainly helped. Nonetheless, Darcy was about fed up Brasiliat's data gathering, if you wanted to call it that. They should have already been at the ore site and in the process of setting up camp for the evening. Unlike Sergeant Lesniak's squad, Darcy's wouldn't be returning to base camp until the camp at the ore site was set up and the area around it fully secured.

Brasiliat was kneeling next to an old tree and appeared to be checking out its massive roots which protruded up through the forest floor. As Darcy approached him, the scout looked up at him with a rather grim expression.

"We're being watched," Brasiliat informed him.

"By who?" Darcy asked, laughing.

"Not by who, but by what," Brasiliat corrected him. "And don't ask, I have no idea. I just know whatever they are, they've been with us all day."

Darcy saw that Brasiliat was serious. "Is that so?"

Brasiliat nodded. "Have you been paying attention to the readings on that hand-scanner you're carrying?" Without giving Darcy a chance to answer, he added, "I'd wager you've been picking up quite a few odd magnetic disturbances on it, haven't you?"

Darcy nodded, admitting that he had. "So what?"

"I believe our new *friends* are travelling the pathways of this planet and those disturbances are a direct result of their using them."

"I thought psycho-portation didn't leave telltale signs," Darcy argued.

Brasiliat grunted. "Everything leaves something by which you can track it, Sergeant, even what I do. I can feel them moving about every time one of those disturbances occurs."

Darcy frowned. "Do think maybe what you're feeling is just you being paranoid? I mean, come on. We haven't seen a single sign of animal life or anything other than green so far."

"Think about what you just said," Brasiliat countered. "A world like this should be teeming with animal life, shouldn't it?"

Darcy glanced around at the lush forest surrounding them and knew Brasiliat was right. "And your theory about why there are no animals…"

"Didn't say I had one," Brasiliat shrugged, "I said we're being watched."

Darcy tapped his helmet's comm. "Base camp, can you read me? Over."

"What are you doing?" Brasiliat asked.

"What does it look like I'm doing?" Darcy scowled. "I'm trying to get in touch with Colonel Stone."

"You haven't been checking in?" Brasiliat stared at him.

"Haven't been able to the last few miles," Darcy explained. "Something is wrong with the signal."

Brasiliat stood up. "Get your men together. We need to get out of here."

"Now hold on, Brasiliat," Darcy started, but he never got the chance to finish. A creature, covered in black fur with wings folded beneath its arms, appeared behind the sergeant. Darcy grunted as blood exploded from his chest to splatter over Brasiliat. Brasiliat could see the thing's clawed hand protruding from the sergeant's chest that it had punched through.

The creature was fast. It flung Darcy's corpse from its arm and sprang at Brasiliat, but the scout was faster. Both of his pistols were drawn to meet it as it came. They cracked in rapid succession as Brasiliat put six rounds into the creature's arms and chests. Black blood flew from the wounds, but the bullets did nothing to slow the monster. Brasiliat slid into the pathways of the planet, stepping out of them behind that thing that had killed Darcy. He could hear gunfire and screams from the woods around him and knew the rest of the squad had been engaged by the creatures as well.

Brasiliat aimed his next barrage of fire carefully, popping off another six rounds at the black-furred thing in front of him. It had turned towards the spot he had appeared as if it knew where that spot would be. Man and monster exchanged a fleeting, half second of mutual surprise before the shots from Brasiliat's pistols blew the creature's skull into chunks of flying bone.

"Frag!" Brasiliat cursed. The screams and gunfire amid the trees had already grown silent. He took a deep breath, centered his mind, and blinked himself away into nothingness.

****

Captain Merrick felt the explosion that blew out a section of the *Vanguard*'s lower decks, flinging himself forward in his command chair with a sharp grunt. He was fully merged with the ship's systems now and had opted to personally join in the battle against the unexpected boarders. The *Vanguard*'s internal cameras and sensors had become his eyes. He watched helplessly as one of the monsters moved along a corridor with blinding speed, slaying every crewman unlucky enough to wander into its path.

In another section of the ship, he saw a trio of security officers trying to hold the monsters back. The creatures were working their way systemically towards the *Vanguard*'s bridge, killing everyone in their path. He could hear the sound of the security officers' gunfire in his mind through his link with the ship. Their rifles chattered on full-auto. The noise was deafening in the confined space of the corridor, and yet the screeches of pure fury from the bat-like monsters overpowered it. One of the monsters stumbled as high-velocity rounds ripped and tore at its upper body. The monster unfolded its thick, hairy wings and began to use them as shields against the continued onslaught. Another of the monsters came flying over it, skimming the corridor's ceiling to strike at the security officers. It would have landed in their center, all claws, teeth, and anger, except that one of the officers was carrying a multi-barreled mini-RPG launcher. The officer slung the weapon upwards at the creature, squeezing its trigger. The RPG the weapon fired streaked to meet the monster, blowing it apart in an explosion that shook the corridor and damaged its walls. The explosion knocked two of the officers from their feet and slammed the monster using its wings as shields, hard, into the corridor wall with the sound of shattering bones. It lay on the corridor floor, black blood seeping from its mouth in long strands like drool, its head twisted in an unnatural angle at the top of its neck.

As the security officers scrambled to their feet, more of the creatures rounded the bend of the corridor. None of the creatures had eyes, Merrick realized, though it appeared at one time their race did have them. The sockets were still present on their faces but overgrown with dense flesh which only added to the hideousness of their appearance. The creatures strongly resembled Earth bats and their ears were wildly overgrown pointed affairs that rose from the sides of their heads. Merrick wondered if the creatures used sound to track their prey or some other unseen means.

The one security officer who had remained on his feet after the explosion in the corridor poured fire into the fastest of the approaching monsters, but the creature wasn't even slowed by it. Chunks of flesh were blown from its body and black blood splattered the corridor walls, but still the thing came on. It landed in front of the officer, taking point-blank fire to its chest. Before it died though, a single swipe of one of its clawed hands cut deep grooves from the bottom to the top of the officer's face and sent his suddenly lifeless body flying. Merrick knew the creature had sacrificed itself so that those behind it would be able to sweep over the remaining two officers, and so they did. The men died screaming, victims of a feral and frenzied rage.

Merrick directed the ship's system to close off the corridor by sealing its blast doors on both ends. The heavy doors slid into place, trapping the three monsters in the corridor… Or at least that had been his intent. The monsters raced to the closer of the two doors and began pounding on it with their fists. Their blows fell like sledgehammers upon the thick metal, denting it time and time again. Sparks flew as one of the creatures opted to use its claws on the door. Merrick felt each blow and slash that struck the door. He had to pull his mind out of that portion of the *Vanguard* so that pain wouldn't cause him to black out. Still, his mind raced on from one section of the ship to another, watching those under his command die as he did what he could to help them.

A young man who wore the uniform of technician ran for his life from one of the monsters in an aft section of the ship. Merrick could see that the monster was going to overtake him easily unless he was able to do something to stop it or buy the young ensign time to reach the lift he was darting towards. Reaching out with his mind, Merrick caused the lift doors to open ahead of the young ensign and activated the corridor's fire suppression system. White chemical foam erupted from the roof of the corridor over the monster. It screeched in confusion, twisting about beneath the deluge. The second it took for the monster to realize that the foam was harmless to it was enough. The doors to the lift closed behind the young ensign as he dashed into it. The victory was perhaps a small one, but it gave Merrick hope.

The *Vanguard* drew Merrick's attention to her engine room as the power there spiked. His awareness entered the room, merged with the ship's systems there. At once, he realized what had caused the surge. A security officer, doing her best to protect an injured member of the engineering staff, had blasted one of the monsters with an automatic shotgun and sent it reeling into a conduit that shunted power from the ship's main reactor to her shields. Merrick sensed the ship's shields failing even as the monster danced and jerked about against the damaged and broken conduit like a human who was being electrocuted. There was no system that allowed Merrick to smell the thing's burning hair and meat, but he could imagine it just the same.

The security officer was trying her best to get the injured engineer to his feet and help him towards the closest exit, but Merrick's awareness told him that many more of the monsters were on their way towards the pair. He had to make a choice between attempting to aid the two of them or protect the *Vanguard*'s main reactor. In the end, it wasn't a choice at all but merely duty that needed to be carried out. He closed off the engineering section with every door that he could seal between it and the monsters throughout the ship. In the process, he trapped those two poor souls between two blast doors with one of the monsters trapped inside the small area with them. His mental presence didn't linger to see what become of the officer and the crewman she was trying to protect. Not even he could be everywhere at once, and there were so many more places within the ship that needed his attention.

Merrick sent his awareness hurtling through the ship towards her hangar bay. He touched it just long enough to see that the hangar had become an open warzone, as many of his crew had headed there in their panicked attempt to flee the monsters. Most of those in the hangar were not armed and those that were clutched only pistols and small arms likely looted from the interior of emergency kits housed in the bay's remaining two dropships. The images he received of the bay were brief and only a glimpse at best because he was jarred back into his body.

Sweat soaked Merrick's hair as his eyes snapped open, and he found himself still sitting in his command chair on the bridge. The rough hands of Berkman, the ranking officer of the security he had summoned to defend the bridge earlier, were shaking him.

"Captain!" Berkman was yelling at him. "We have to go, sir!"

It was difficult to take in what was happening around after his prolonged mental merger with the *Vanguard.* As he forced himself to focus on the physical world surrounding his body, he heard the whine of metal being bent inward as clawed hands tore through the door of the bridge's lift.

"They're going to get in here, sir!" Berkman shouted. "We can't stop them!"

Merrick allowed Berkman to jerk him up from his command chair to his feet.

"Which way?" Merrick muttered, the shock he was feeling clear in his expression.

The lift's door exploded onto the bridge as it gave way to the fury of the monsters attacking it from inside the lift's shaft and the monsters poured onto the bridge, half a dozen strong.

****

Berkman led Merrick into the ready room that adjoined the bridge. The lift that the monsters had entered the bridge through was its only real entrance and exit. Merrick didn't blame Berkman for not wanting to gamble on trying to escape via maintenance. Such a move would have brought more risks than its payoff was worth. Merrick knew full well just how widespread through the *Vanguard* the monsters from the planet were now. If he, Berkman, and the other security officers trying to protect him encountered the monsters in the enclosed space of one those shafts, there wouldn't be much room to fight back in, and they would likely all be slaughtered very quickly.

Two of Berkman's men remained on the bridge trying to protect the bridge crew. Berkman and another officer Merrick believed was named Clint sealed the doors of the ready room. A mixture of gunfire, screams of pain and terror, and the horrific screeches and howls of the monsters could be heard on the other side of them.

"Help me!" Berkman shouted at Clint who was looking as shocked and dazed as Merrick felt. Berkman was straining to shove Merrick's desk up to the ready room's door to help bar it.

"Clint, man, come on!" Berkman yelled again and Clint shook his head, snapping into action. The two security officers got the desk moved to block the door. Then Berkman and Clint ravaged the ready room, adding anything else they could that had weight to the desk, creating a makeshift barricade to block the monsters' way.

"It won't hold them," Merrick commented in an utterly detached voice. "I've seen them tear through a lot tougher stuff."

Berkman ignored him. "Clint, get over there!" Berkman pointed to the right of the door. "I'll cover it from the left."

Merrick could see that they were taking up firing positions to get the best angle they could against the monsters when they came through the barricaded door, and they would. It was only a matter of time.

Retreating to the rear of the ready room, Merrick slumped against the wall there. It was unthinkable that a ship like the *Vanguard* could be taken by such primitive and animal-like beings that monsters were. In truth, the entire mess was unthinkable. Every report on Talia II had said the same: *No indigenous, higher lifeforms. No threat of any kind.* Clearly, those reports had been wrong, and now they were all paying the price for it.

"Sir!" Berkman shouted at him from the position he had taken to the right of the ready room door. "Is there anything you can do to help us?"

Merrick shook his head sadly. He was a telemechanic, not a warrior. He was trained for to captain a ship and lead her into the heart of space battle where nukes flew among the stars of the void. His level of this sort of combat extended to a mere two weeks in Boot many years gone by.

Berkman drew the sidearm he carried in a holster on his hip and tossed it at him. Merrick caught the weapon.

"Try, sir!" Berkman told him. "When those things come through the door, aim for their heads and be frag sure not to hit me or Clint over there when you do!"

Merrick nodded his understanding, but he set the pistol on the floor next to him. There were more important things he needed to attend to. He blocked out Berkman's shouting at Clint as the two of them got ready for the monsters, and the pounding on the ready room's door began in earnest, hurling his awareness once more into the *Vanguard*'s systems.

****

Lieutenant Mat Spraker crouched behind the cover of a stack of crates sitting near one of the two dropships left in the *Vanguard*'s hangar. His count put the number of monsters in the hangar at over two dozen with more guarding the hangar's exits. *Where had they all come from?* he wondered. The things had appeared out of nowhere to run amok on the ship. The only possible explanation was that were psycho-porters of the highest order.

Corpses littered the floor of the hangar, and still, the killing went on. Over a hundred of the ship's crew had ended up here and were now making their last stand against the monsters. The monsters controlled the only routes of escape and approaching them ensured one a quick death.

Spraker had tried to organize those he could when he first arrived before the all-out attack from the monsters began. There had been so little time. At the start of it all, after he had led the others in looting the dropships and leftover supplies from the loading of the dropships that had long departed for the planet below, he had been able to arm nearly thirty of the gathered crew.

Those arms had been mostly pistols with a few scattered rifles mixed in. It all seemed pointless to Spraker as he stared at a dead man who lay a couple of yards from where he was hiding. The hand he had clutched his pistol with was gone. In its place was a bloody stump. One of the monsters had sliced the man's hand from the end of his arm with its claws before proceeding to gut the man in front of Spraker. Strands of bloated, red-slicked purple snakes that were the man's intestines spilled onto the hangar floor around his corpse.

A nearby scream tore Spraker gaze away from the man's corpse. He peeked around the edge of the stack of crates to see Ensign Mendez running for her life from one of the monsters. Every rational instinct within him told him not to try to help her, but he knew he couldn't just sit back and watch another of the crew die.

Spraker leaped to his feet, taking aim at the monster where it soared above Ensign Mendez, circling her as it prepared to swoop in for the kill. He had found a tank-killer cannon aboard one of the dropships and claimed it for himself during the looting. The weapon looked like a giant barreled shotgun. It contained only four rounds, of which he had already fired two. It was meant to be fired in full combat gear. Even with the weapon's own heavy recoil suppression system, the shoulder he braced it against was bruised to the bone from his earlier two shots. A third might break the bone beneath his flesh. Spraker didn't see that he had a choice though. He took aim at the monster. The shot echoed throughout the hangar above the cacophony of the battle or, better put, *massacre*, that continued around him. Spraker cursed and gritted his teeth against the pain as the bones of his shoulder were shattered by the tank-killer's kick. His aim was true though. The monster never knew what hit it. One second it was there, swooping downwards at Ensign Mendez, and the next, a rain of pulped meat and black blood splashed over her.

Stumbling, Spraker collapsed to his knees. He had saved Mendez's life at the cost of drawing the attention of all the monsters in the hangar onto himself. A monster blinked into existence directly in front of him. Two more appeared, one to his right, another behind him. Spraker was smiling as the three of them grabbed hold of him at once and pulled his body in different directions. Flesh and bone gave way to enraged, animal strength as Spraker's blood joined with that of the already dead on the hangar's floor.

****

Brasiliat toppled out of the pathway he had used to escape the grizzly massacre of Darcy's men. The taint infecting the pathway sickened him as he fell, face first, into the grass outside of the entrance to Alpha I. Brasiliat looked up at the massive APC and breathed a sigh of relief. He had made it back to Colonel Stone and the unit's basecamp.

What seemed like chaos reigned around him as men and women went running about, carrying out their orders. There was thankfully, however, no sign that the camp was under attack. Brasiliat hurled himself to his feet. Through Alpha I's open side door, he could see Colonel Stone inside it. Several of those hurrying about paused to stare at him as he did so. One called out, offering help, but Brasiliat ignored her.

"Stone!" he yelled as he stumbled into Alpha I.

"Brasiliat!" Stone exclaimed at the sight of him. "What in the devil happened out there?"

There were others inside the rear of APC with her. Brasiliat saw Barnes, a man who could only be Alpha I's driver, and the *Vanguard*'s telepath, Noel. He kept his attention fixed on Stone though.

"Darcy and his men are dead," Brasiliat said coldly. "There are creatures using the pathways of this planet and space around it to move about without being seen. And trust me, Colonel, their intentions are hostile." He waved his hand at Darcy's blood on his uniform.

"We've just become aware of the situation ourselves, Brasiliat," Colonel Stone said.

"Then you know we need to leave this place. Now!" Brasiliat told her.

"We can't," Colonel Stone said in a strained voice. "The *Vanguard* is under attack too."

Her words hit Brasiliat like a runaway truck, nearly knocking him to the ground from the shock of them thanks to the weakness he was still feeling from his last blink through the corrupted pathways of Talia II.

Barnes moved to help him, but Brasiliat shoved the precog away from him. "Get your hands off of me, Barnes!" he snapped. Recovering and standing upright again, Brasiliat glared at Stone. "How bad is it?"

Colonel Stone shrugged. "We don't know. The last report from Captain Merrick sounded rather…grim. He didn't order us to remain on the planet, but I got the feel that he wanted us to."

"Then we need to get ready here," Brasiliat growled.

"I've already given orders to do just that, Brasiliat," Stone said, her cheeks flushed with anger at the scout's suggestion that she hadn't.

"These *things* aren't us, Colonel," Brasiliat argued. "They don't think like we do."

"He's right," Noel chimed in.

"We can't expect them to act like the enemies we are used to dealing with," Brasiliat continued. "If we follow the SOPs, we'll all be dead before the sun rises tomorrow."

"Are you saying you know how these creatures think?" Colonel Stone asked with a questioning expression of disbelief.

"No, ma'am," Brasiliat answered. "I am saying I know how they'll attack when they do."

Brasiliat paused, choosing his words carefully. "And I believe I will be able to feel them ahead of where they will appear as well."

Colonel Stone nodded. "Because you travel the pathways too."

"Exactly, ma'am. No matter how alien their minds may be, those of us with the gift of psycho-portation all develop a pattern of how we use it whether we are conscious of that pattern or not."

"You're charge of the basecamp's defense then, Brasiliat. Don't make me regret it," Colonel Stone cautioned him.

Brasiliat darted out of Alpha I, shouting orders at the men and women who were preparing for battle.

"You believe him then," Barnes commented.

"I think that man is likely the best hope any of us have right now of making off this planet alive, Barnes," Colonel Stone said firmly.

"He truly meant what he said about being able to feel them," Noel added. "I've touched their minds, and if their those things present in the pathways of this world are anything like the horror I experienced from that contact, there's no chance someone as plugged into the pathways as he is couldn't feel them."

McGregor burst into laughter. "Feeling your own gift is a touch useless, eh, mate?"

Barnes whirled on the APC driver. "Watch yourself, Specialist. You're speaking to a superior officer."

McGregor raised his hands in mock surrender, "Just call them as I see them, mate."

"Gentlemen," Colonel Stone spoke up, a tone of warning in her voice. "While Brasiliat is out there trying to save our butts, I think it's best that we focus on the big picture. Establishing contact with the *Vanguard* is the first step in seeing what that picture is going to look like. Noel?"

"I know what you're about to ask of me, Colonel, and the answer is no. I am not strong enough to reach Captain Merrick's mind from down here. The distance is just too great." Noel shook her head sadly.

"Take a seat somewhere, get yourself focused, and try anyway," Colonel Stone ordered.

"Yes, ma'am." Noel headed for a corner of the APC's rear away from where the others stood so she could be a bit more alone for the attempt she'd been ordered to make.

"McGregor!" Colonel Stone roared.

"Yes, ma'am?" he asked, stunned by her anger.

"Why are you still standing here?" she urged him.

"No idea, ma'am," he answered and dove for the driver compartment of Alpha I. Its door slid shut behind him, leaving Barnes facing her alone.

There was still a smug look on Barnes' face as Colonel Stone looked over at him.

"You *have* been utterly useless so far, Barnes. McGregor was right in calling you on that." She kept her voice level and professional. "I suggest you work on changing that."

"How?" Barnes croaked. "What do you want me to do? Scan the future again right now while we're standing here?"

"That wouldn't be a bad idea," Colonel Stone grinned, "and for all our sakes, I hope whatever you see has some truth to it this time around."

****

Sergeant Lesniak ran for his life. Ford was ahead of him, cutting through the trees in a panicked dash. The two of them were the only survivors of Lesniak's squad. They'd been hit, hard and fast, by monsters that seemed to have crawled out of the darkest of nightmares. Every so often, one of the monsters would appear in their path or to come swooping down on them from the sky above. So far, they had been lucky. That was really the truth of it. Otherwise, they would have been dead already.

They had killed several of the monsters, each time hoping it was the last of the things. It never was. Lesniak hadn't been able to reach Colonel Stone at the unit's basecamp or even the *Vanguard* in orbit around Talia II for some time. Something was blocking the comm.'s signal. He had no idea what that something could be. He wasn't a tech. Lesniak was a ground pounder to his very bones.

The one thing he excelled at in life was death, and that talent was paying off for him.

One of the monsters blinked into existence in front of him, grabbing at Ford from behind. Lesniak had no time to use his triple-barreled shotgun, so he reached out with his telekinesis, lifting the monster from where it stood to bash it against the tree it had appeared next to. He saw one of the monster's arms snap from the impact and the white of bone come sticking through the black hair that covered the creature's body and its flesh. The creature gave a shriek of pain and was gone as instantaneously as it had appeared. Ford had to have heard it all, but the man didn't slow a single step. He kept right on running as fast as he could.

Lesniak knew they were both on the verge of collapse. The running battle to reach the unit's basecamp was taking its toll on them. They needed to come up with a new plan and fast, or they were dead. As he and Ford ran on, Lesniak kept his eyes peeled for anywhere they make be able to take shelter and make a proper stand against the monsters, maybe drive them off. Ammo was becoming an issue, but he figured they might have just enough to bloody the monsters to the point where they pulled back if they could just find somewhere to do it.

Another monster appeared so close to Lesniak he could smell the putrid stench of the thing's breath on him. The only thing that saved him from the monster slicing his head from his shoulders was his instincts. A deeper part of his mind than his conscious one erected a telekinetic shield about him at the last second. The monster's claws sparked against it instead of cutting into his throat. Even so, the impact of the blow sent Lesniak reeling. He stumbled, trying to regain his balance as the monster came at him again. Lesniak raised a hand towards it, hitting the monster with a concentrated blast of telekinetic force that smashed the bones inside its body to bits. The monster's corpse flew backwards several yards from Lesniak, its corpse landing, broken, on the grass of the forest floor.

"That was a close one, Sarge," Ford commented. Ford had realized that Lesniak was in danger and whirled about to lend what aid he could. "How many more of those things can there be?"

"A planet full," Lesniak grumbled. "Just keep moving!"

The path through the trees had opened up some. The two men now ran side by side. A chorus of screeching voices drew their attention to the sky. Dozens of the monsters flew above them, circling them as they ran onwards towards the unit's basecamp.

"God have mercy on us," Ford panted.

The muscles of Lesniak's legs burned with every step he took, and Ford looked half-dead. Both of their uniforms were soaked through with sweat and stained with the black blood of the monsters they had killed during their running battle. Lesniak winced as he watched Ford trip over something in the grass and go rolling, his body bouncing over the grass. He couldn't tell if Ford had been injured in the fall or not, but Ford wasn't moving. That was a very bad thing as his fall gave the monsters above them the push to press their advantage. Half a dozen of the monsters came swooping downwards at the fallen soldier. Lesniak blew the first of them apart with a simultaneous burst of all three of his shotgun's barrels. Even as he pumped fresh rounds into his weapon's chambers, he knew he wasn't going to be able to stop them with his shotgun. Skidding to a halt, Lesniak focused what remained of his willpower, concentrating it all into one vicious telekinetic attack. Nano-thin blades of telekinetic energy formed in the air between the monsters and where Ford lay. Lesniak sent them spinning into the descending monsters. The five remaining monsters swooping downwards hit the blades like meat being tossed into a grinder. Body parts flew in every direction as black blood fell like rain. Lesniak heard the monsters' startled cries of pain and allowed himself a smile. The other six of the things kept their current altitude and continued to circle over the clearing above Ford, but none of them were brave enough to make a move after seeing their brothers hacked to bits by an invisible force.

It was taking everything Lesniak had left just to stay conscious, but he made it to Ford's side, kneeling next to his friend. Ford's body was face down in the grass. Lesniak reached out to roll Ford over. Ford came awake as he did.

"Did we get them, Sarge?" Ford rasped, staring up at him.

"We got some of them, yeah," Lesniak told him. "Now get the frag on your feet, soldier. I may need you to carry me."

Lesniak knew his surprise butchering of so many of the monsters had given the others pause, but that was sure to wear off, and fast. He tried to help Ford up but nearly collapsed instead. It was Ford who helped him to his feet and tossed one of his arms about his shoulders.

"Come on, Sarge," Ford shouted. "Colonel Stone will kill me if I leave your sorry butt behind."

The cries of the monsters above them had grown even more shrill with the promise of violence. Lesniak looked up in the sky and saw the monsters preparing to make another move at them.

"Sarge!" Ford yelled, pointing ahead of them. "Look!"

Lesniak did and couldn't believe what he saw. The very fabric of reality itself was torn apart ahead of them. A glowing portal formed in their path. Brasiliat emerged from it, his custom pistols drawn. The scout opened fire on the monsters in the sky as they swept downwards.

"The colonel sent me to bring you guys home!" Brasiliat shouted over the booming of his pistols. "Get the Hades through that gate already! I can't hold it forever!"

Lesniak was flung through the gate by Ford as his world went black.

****

The *Vanguard* was lost. Captain Merrick's awareness coursed through the ship's system, desperately straining to find a means of saving her. The unexpected and brutal attack by the bat-like creatures that had come out of nowhere was something no one could have anticipated or been ready for. Never in his career had he heard of such an attack. Among humans, though there were a growing number of those born with psionic abilities, psycho-portation was one of the rarest. This race of bat-like monsters, however, it seemed had evolved with psycho-portative abilities being a natural part of who and what they were.

Most of the *Vanguard*'s crew was dead. All those lives lost, and for what? Merrick wondered. Another world for the human race to ravage? Guilt clawed at his heart and soul. He had lead the mission to Talia II, and their blood was on him just as much as it was on the powers that be back home. Rationally, he understood that there was nothing he could have done differently that would have made any difference, but that didn't matter when stacked against the grief and loss he felt.

Now he had to weigh the lives of those who remained and those who were on the planet below against the greater good. The *Vanguard* was not the only ship that had been dispatched for Talia II. The *Seeder* wasn't that far behind her.

Merrick considered blowing the *Vanguard*, an easy thing to do for a telemechanic. That option wasn't a good one though. He wasn't concerned about human tech falling into the hands of the bat creatures. They didn't seem anywhere near on the level of being able to make use of it. What he was concerned about were those aboard the colony ship and Colonel Stone's unit on the planet below. When the attack had begun, he had ordered the two dropships that had dispatched Colonel Stone's unit to the surface of Talia II not to return to the *Vanguard*. They had taken up positions in orbit on the other side of the planet from the *Vanguard* and were still out there too. Neither of them had reported coming under attack from the bat creatures as yet.

Accessing the ship's comm. system, Merrick sent them an encrypted file of their new orders over a secure channel. He doubted the bats were listening in, but SOPs and common sense were ingrained in who he was. It was always better to be safe than sorry.

With the orders to the two dropships dispatched, Merrick accessed the *Vanguard*'s missile launchers, firing a drone carrying a download of the ship's logs into space aimed at the path of the *Seeder*. With any luck, the colony ship would intercept the drone and at least not be caught off guard by the bat creatures like he and his crew had been.

He realized he had made his choice about what to do without even realizing it. Merrick accessed two final systems, the

Vanguard's life support controls and her main operational one. He shut down life support through the great warship and then blew several of her interior hatches that led into space. Her atmosphere would bleed into the stars and she would freeze, becoming a place that the bats couldn't possibly survive in a very short time. Doing so would also leave her where she could be retrieved by either the crew of the *Seeder* or Colonel Stone's unit on the planet below once the dropships returned to her basecamp.

Merrick had just finished his work when his mind was jerked back into the psychical by the sound of metal being rendered and the screeching cries of the bat-like monsters that had just ripped their way into the ready room where he, Berkman, and Clint had taken refuge. Berkman and Clint opened fire on the monsters with their rifles as Merrick snatched up the pistol that rested beside him on the floor. Merrick readied the pistol and moved to join them.

The first few creatures through the door were shredded into masses of mangled meat by the combined fire of Berkman and Clint. The monsters kept coming though as if there was no end to their number. Berkman's rifle clicked empty. Merrick did his best to pick up the slack and hold the doorway, emptying his pistol's mag. into monsters. He killed two for his efforts: the first with a barrage of shots that took it down just from their quantity and a second with a lucky shot that slammed home directly inside the thing's flesh-covered eye socket.

Berkman had reloaded and resumed firing at the monsters spilling through the doorway. Clint was in the process of reloading now though.

"Mag.!" Merrick shouted at the younger security officer, knowing that all his security personnel were required to carry more than just the one inside of their own sidearm even when the ship wasn't being threatened. Not to mention the fact that when he had called their squad to the bridge, Berkman and his men had arrived geared up for heavy combat.

Either Clint couldn't hear him over the sound of the gunfire and screeching of the monsters in the enclosed room, or he was too focused on holding the doorway to care about his order. Merrick could see that the young officer didn't have the time to toss him one anyway. There was a growing pile of monster corpses at the door of the ready room, but still the things came on, more determined than ever to get at him and the two security officers. They got the opening they had been pressing for as Berkman's rifle clicked empty again. Though Clint cut two of the monsters down, several more got through.

One of them charged directly at Berkman, reaching him to rip his rifle from his hands and fling it across the ready room. Merrick saw Berkman go for his sidearm and the look of horror that washed over his face as he remembered it was gone. That one slip of memory or perhaps instinct cost Berkman his life. The monster grabbed him up by his throat. The claws of its hand dug deep into the flesh of his neck as the claws of its other hand sliced opened his body from his groin to his sternum. Blood and organs oozed from Berkman's cut open body to the floor below where he dangled in the monster's grasp.

"Berkman!" Clint screamed as he fired his rifle, point blank, into a monster that came charging at him. The high-velocity rounds blew massive holes in the monster and it died as it reached him. Clint sidestepped its collapsing form, trying to bring his rifle to bear on those behind it as Merrick watched on helplessly. Two of the monsters knocked Clint to the floor of the ready room and descended upon on him in a berserker-style rage. Blood flew as their claws ravaged his struggling form.

Weaponless and with nowhere to run, Merrick did the only thing he could. He stood his ground proudly with defiance blazing in his eyes and his fists clenched as the monsters came from him. He could only hope his death would be a quick one…and it was.

****

Sergeant Lesniak woke up screaming. Sweat slicked his skin as he grabbed at the person standing over him. Whoever it was had quick reflexes. They blocked his attempt to grab them and pinned his arm back to his chest. No small feat given the bulging muscles of his thick arms.

"Sergeant!" Colonel Stone shouted at him as her face came into focus and he realized who was holding him.

Lesniak stopped fighting against her as he looked around and saw that he was lying in the rear compartment of one his unit's two APCs. "Sorry, ma'am," he said. The last thing he remembered was Brasiliat showing up to save his butt and Ford flinging him into the open maw of one of the Brasiliat's psionically generated doorways.

"You're safe now, or rather as safe as anyone can be on this fragging planet," Colonel Stone told him. "I need you on your feet, Sergeant, so I hope you've gotten the rest you needed."

"How long have I been out, ma'am?" Lesniak asked, sitting up, and sliding his combat-booted feet from the bench he rested on the APC's metal floor.

"A few hours." Colonel Stone shrugged. "I don't recall exactly. A lot has happened since you took your squad out, Sergeant."

"Ford?" Lesniak blurted out as he thought of how the others of his squad had been ripped apart by the alien bat-like creatures that traveled the planet's pathways like Brasiliat.

"He's fine," Colonel Stone assured him. "He's outside helping get basecamp ready for the attack that is surely coming."

"The bats," Lesniak stated more than asked.

Colonel Stone nodded. "I've put Brasiliat in charge of the camp's defense, but I need you out there too, Lesniak. You're one of the best weapons I have at my disposal right now. Get geared up. I expect the attack will be coming sooner than any of us would like."

Lesniak moved to one of the APC's small weapon lockers and started loading up with all the ammo he could carry. "Is Captain Merrick sending support from the *Vanguard*, ma'am?"

Colonel Stone frowned. "When we last heard from Captain Merrick and the *Vanguard*, Sergeant, the ship was under attack. We've heard nothing more since that time. The *Vanguard* could very well be lost."

Sergeant Lesniak stared at her for a moment, his mind processing what she had just told him before he spoke. "So we're on our own then?"

"Aren't we always, Lesniak?" Colonel Stone answered darkly.

"Understood, ma'am." He nodded as he finished gearing up.

"We have to hold this camp, Sergeant," Colonel Stone said firmly. "During the time you were out, we received an encrypted message from the two dropships that brought us down here. They never returned to the *Vanguard*. Captain Merrick ordered them to remain in orbit on the other side of the planet. Lieutenant Farrell, who's their ranking officer, says he plans on doing a pass by the *Vanguard* to see what kind of shape she's in and then will be joining us here on the surface. The ETA of the dropships is oh six hundred hours."

Lesniak glanced at his chronometer. "So five hours then?"

"Five hours if we're able to hold this camp and be here when they arrive," Colonel Stone corrected him.

"Have we learned anything more about the bat creatures? How many there are? Where they're all coming from?" Lesniak asked.

"They are apparently a somewhat primitive race that is indigenous to Talia II. We have to assume that they vastly outnumber us, and as you've seen firsthand, they are psychoporters of the highest order, all of them. Whether the creatures are attacking us because we have threatened their territory or are merely aggressive by nature, I've got no clue. Both our telepaths, Noel and Brasiliat, believe the creatures to be intelligent, though they don't appear to be technologically inclined. There's been no sign of them using any kind of weapons, and our sensors don't detect any power sources on this planet. Of course, that doesn't really mean anything. We had no idea that the creatures were even here until they made their presence known."

Us against a planet, Lesniak thought. *That sounds about like how it normally goes.*

Lesniak started for the APC's open side door, but Colonel Stone called after him.

"Sergeant." She grinned at him. "Kill as many of those fraggers as you can. Do I make myself clear?'

"As crystal." Lesniak nodded, grinning back at her.

****

Sergeant Lesniak stepped out of APC Alpha I. He spotted Brasiliat in the gunner's turret of Alpha II, tapping his comm.

"Hey, Brasiliat," he called. "Thanks for the save, man."

He and Ford both owed their lives to the scout. If he hadn't appeared when he did to whisk them back to basecamp, they would be bat food right now.

"I've set up a grid around the basecamp using modified, mounted sensors," Brasiliat answered him, all business. "If you flip your helmet's visor in place, you should be able to see what I mean."

Lesniak did so. What he saw resembled something akin to infra-red only instead of detecting temps, he figured it was detecting disturbances in the planet's magnetic field. *Clever*, he thought. Leave it to Brasiliat to come with something so unconventional. If it worked as the scout intended though, it would help a lot to level the playing field when the bats made their move. Lesniak wasn't a scientist or psycho-porter, but he wasn't stupid either. He knew what Brasiliat was going for. In the moment before one of the bats emerged from the planet's pathways, the sensors should show the magnetic field of that area fluctuating.

Mourning the loss of his tri-barrel shotgun, Lesniak had opted for a more standard-issue automatic one. The unit had very few of them, as most troopers preferred assault rifles to shotguns. Lesniak checked the weapon's mag. and readied it for action. An attack from the bats could come at any time. Night had fallen over the basecamp. There were lighting modules spread out around the camp. They added to ambient light of the stars above, not that it mattered. Lesniak was sure that every single trooper not inside one of the two APCs was looking at the world through their helmets' visors, alert for any sign of the bats. Everyone was in position too, hunkered down behind supply crates, lying flat in the grass decked-out in camo, or using the APCs themselves as cover. Lesniak looked over them as he found a spot of his own. He frowned at what he saw. Most of the troopers were settled in as if they were expecting a firefight and not the kind of attack the bats were going to be bringing them. The bats, as yet, hadn't even used anything as simple as a crossbow much less guns. Their way of fighting was based entirely around their ability to teleport. They liked to get in close, surprising their target if possible, strike, and port away. Lesniak hoped the other soldiers were ready for that, but he doubted it. If he hadn't already had a prolonged engagement with the bats, he doubted he would have been either.

Lesniak was still walking across the camp towards the spot he had chosen for his cover when it all hit the fan. One second, the night was quiet and still. The next, there were disturbances everywhere in the magnetic field. The warning from the sensors that Brasiliat had set up flooded his visor with the arrival positions of too many targets for him to even try to count. Lesniak picked one of the disturbances and took aim at it. Sure enough, a bat appeared there half a second later. His automatic shotgun blazed as he squeezed its trigger. The bat was dead by the time it was fully out of the pathway it was traveling through. Its body, mangled by the heavy slugs from his shotgun, dropped from the air like a ton of bricks to crash into the grass.

The night was lit by muzzle flashes as every trooper in the camp opened fire, their weapons blazing away at the appearing bats. The roof cannons of the two APCs thundered, spinning on their axis to engage one bat after another. The bats that took hits from the cannons died instantly, their bodies blown apart into flying bits of the remnants of arms and legs, chunks of nearly pulped organs and bone fragments. Alpha II's cannon fired at a faster rate than Alpha I, and Lesniak knew that was because Brasiliat was manning it himself. He didn't need to wait for the mounted sensors to tell him where the bats would be appearing. The scout could feel them before they were even detected by the sensors he had placed around the camp.

Dozens upon dozens of bats died in those first seconds of the engagement, so many that the attack suddenly stopped as quickly as it had begun. Lesniak couldn't believe it. They had bloodied the monsters so badly that they had given the things pause, a feat that had seemed impossible to him as he knew just how willing the bats were to sacrifice themselves in order to allow another member of their race to get in and do real damage to their target.

Brasiliat's voice came over his comm. using the unit's open channel so that everyone could hear him, shouting, "It's not over. This is just a pause in the storm. Stay ready."

Lesniak figured the scout was right. The bats had taken a good blow for sure but not enough of one to drive them off for good. Likely, the monsters were thinking right now, reexamining how they were going to hit the basecamp. Brasiliat's play with the sensors had caught them utterly by surprise. Clearly, the bats weren't used to their targets knowing where they were going to appear. Lesniak took a glance at the corpses of the monsters littering the basecamp and its perimeter. *Serves you bastards right,* he thought, laughing.

"Incoming!" Brasiliat shouted over the unit's shared comm. link as Lesniak's visor lit up with targets again. This time, the bats were really getting in close and coming fast. A disturbance formed nearly on top of where Lesniak was standing. He threw himself to the side as a bat appeared right next to him. There was no time to bring his weapon to bear on the monster. Instead, he plunged its butt backwards, slugging the monster in its stomach. It gave a grunt of pain as Lesniak finished turning to face it and was able to bring the butt of his shotgun up in an arc that brought its butt into contact with the monster's lower jaw. Razor-like teeth were shattered as the thing's head was snapped backwards. Lesniak lashed out with a kick meant to send it to the ground, but the bat was gone. Despite the pain his blows had inflicted on it, the monster had retained enough presence of mind to teleport away.

With the bat he had been fighting suddenly gone, Lesniak searched for another target. Private Amberly, off to his left, was locked in combat with a bat of her own. The thing had the clawed fingers of its hands wrapped around the center of her rifle, trying to tear it from her hands. Lesniak jerked up his automatic shotgun and fired a three-round burst into the thing that sent it staggering, black blood oozing from the holes the slugs had blown in its side. Private Amberly finished the thing with the sidearm she jerked from the holster on her hip. Her pistol cracked, putting a hole in the monster's forehead. Her bent and twisted rifle lay at her feet, broken and useless.

Lesniak had no time to shout a warning as he saw a second bat emerge from a pathway behind Private Amberly. He didn't have a clear shot at the thing either unless he was willing to take out Private Amberly in the process. She must have somehow sensed the thing because she started to turn towards it. Before she could even finish whirling about to face it though, the bat took hold of her head with both of its hands and crushed her head, helmet and all, like a rotten melon. Private Amberly's twitching corpse flopped to the ground as the bat vanished. Lesniak's visor nearly blinded him as the magnetic field directly in front of him shifted and the bat emerged, its hands reaching out towards him. Throwing himself backwards, Lesniak barely avoided being snagged by the creature's groping hands. His mind rammed a sliver of telekinetic energy into the bat's skull, slashing through its brains. They erupted from the backside of its skull, splattering outward into the night air.

"Frag me!" Lesniak roared.

****

Safely inside the sealed armor of Alpha I, Barnes was lost to the world. He had no knowledge of the battle that raged outside the vehicle. His mind was adrift in the world of what could be. His body shook and trembled, sweating dripping from him to the APC's floor at his feet. His eyes were rolled up to show only whites and his mouth open in a silent scream.

Noel was already kneeling by his side as Colonel Stone shouted at her from the APC's driver compartment, where the colonel sat beside McGregor, Alpha I's driver. "Help him, Noel!"

Noel, like Barnes, had been focused on using her own gift, trying to telepathically reach Captain Merrick aboard the *Vanguard* in orbit around the planet until the fit Barnes' was having had broken her focus. Her attempt to use her gift had failed, but Barnes was apparently having some success, too much of it in fact. Terrified of what attempting to link to his mind might bring into her own, Noel instead raised her mental shields as touched Barnes's arm and took hold of it.

"Barnes!" she shouted at the precog. "Wake up!"

Barnes began to flop and jerk about in his seat as what he was experiencing became even more intense. Noel wasn't a ground pounder like most of Colonel Stone's unit. She had only come to the surface at Captain Merrick's request. The sound of the battle outside filled her with fear as gunfire intermingled with the pained howls and screeches of the bat creatures. It was hard for her to think clearly when all she wanted to do was hide in a corner of the APC and pray for it all to be over. Colonel Stone and Barnes were counting on her. She might very well be the only chance Barnes had. Noel had heard stories where precogs got so lost in their visions that they became real to them. Those precogs usually either died from the shock of what they were seeing and experiencing or ended up mental vegetables when their glimpse of whatever terrible future they were seeing was over.

Noel hauled back and delivered a backhanded blow to the precog that knocked his head to the side. If Barnes felt it, he gave no sign of it. His body continued to thrash about in his seat, his mouth working as if he were trying to speak though no words were coming out. Not knowing anything else to do, Noel hammered him again. White foam began to bubble out of his parted lips and Noel knew she was losing him. There was no other choice left to her now and she knew it. Noel lowered her shields and reached for Barnes' mind with her. The future came exploding into her mind like a detonating nuke. She screamed at the top of her lungs and then collapsed to the floor of the APC to rest near the precog's kicking feet.

****

The battle still raged around Lesniak as he fired a burst from his automatic shotgun, point blank, into one of the monsters. Its guts splashed over him as the impact of the shotgun's slugs threw the monster away from him. Another bat had already emerged from a pathway to his right, teleporting into the basecamp. Lesniak spun on it as it lashed out at him with its claws. They met the telekinetic field he had surrounded himself in a shower of sparks. Lesniak grunted at the force of the blow but kept his balance. He shoved the barrel of his shotgun up under the monster's chin and blew the thing's brains out the top of its head. Two more bats were moving in on him. One of them exploded in a shower of gore as a blast from Alpha II's roof cannon struck it. Lesniak knew he owed Brasiliat for that. The scout was beginning to make a habit of saving his butt. The other bat came onward, untroubled by the death of its brother. Its mouth was twisted into a snarl as it sprang at him. Lesniak aimed for its head and pulled the trigger, but his automatic shotgun clicked empty. He flung it at the monster, hoping to distract it and buy some time. Instead of merely trying to dodge the weapon though, the monster teleported to only God knows where, giving Lesniak the moment he needed to find his center again.

After the devastating destruction the defenders of the camp had inflicted on the bats during their first attack, the tide of the battle had quickly turned as the second and third waves of bats flooded the camp. There were still more of the creatures dying than colonial marines, but Lesniak wasn't an idiot. He knew that if the tide didn't shift again, and soon, the unit was going to lose and badly.

Lesniak glanced in the direction of Alpha II as the APC's roof cannon went silent. He could see tendrils of smoke rising from the weapon and knew that Brasiliat had finally burnt it out with the rapid shots he had been taking at the appearing waves of bats. It was only a matter of time until Alpha I's overloaded and died as well. As Lesniak watched, Brasiliat blinked out of existence. No doubt the psycho-porting scout was taking the battle to the bats on a more personal level now, teleporter against teleporters. Then Lesniak's time for thinking was done as another bat teleported in, coming at him from his left side. He met it with a telekinetic shove that knocked it off balance as he raised the barrel of his reloaded, automatic shotgun to fire a burst that caved in the monster's chest.

The sound of gunfire was growing quieter with each passing moment as more and more of his unit lost their lives to the claws and teeth of the bats. Alpha I's cannon had fallen silent as well. It hadn't burnt out like Alpha II's, rather several of the bats had appeared around it and ripped it free of its turret. Thankfully, Alpha I's turret was unmanned. The APC's driver, McGregor, had been controlling it from inside the vehicle. Nonetheless, the loss of its firepower was just another step towards the end that was coming to them all if something didn't change and fast.

Brasiliat appeared out of nothingness near him. Lesniak almost crushed the scout's skull with a telekinetic fist but managed to stop himself at the last moment. "Brasiliat! What the...?"

"You're coming with me, Lesniak," Brasiliat yelled and then tackled him like an old Earth football player.

The two of them toppled through the pathway Brasiliat had opened. Reality blurred and bent before Lesniak's eyes. As hardened as he was, Lesniak screamed inside the pathway but there was no sound within it, only cold and a void that alternated between blinding light and utter darkness.

Lesniak crashed onto the floor of Alpha I's rear compartment with Brasiliat on top of him. The scout leaped to his feet, shouting, "I'm here, Colonel!"

"Thank God!" Colonel Stone yelled. The corpses of two bat monsters rested in the doorway to the APC's driver compartment. Not even the vehicle's armored walls could keep the things out, Lesniak realized.

"Keep them out!" Colonel Stone ordered Brasiliat.

Lesniak looked at Brasiliat in awe. "You can do that?"

Brasiliat didn't answer him. His features were twisted into an expression of determined will as he strained to carry out Colonel Stone's orders.

"He can do that," Stone said. "At least for a while."

The two dead bats weren't the only mess in the compartment of Alpha I. Barnes sat slumped over in a pool of urine and sweat, his eyes rolled up in his head to show only whites, looking lost to the world. The telepath, Noel, lay at the precog's feet, not in much better shape herself.

Colonel Stone approached him, grabbing him by the front of his combat suit. "How many of my men are still alive out there?" she spat the question into his face.

"I… I don't know, ma'am," he answered honestly, "not many. I can tell you we need to bug out though before we're completely overrun."

****

Lieutenant Hamilton Farrell read through the encrypted message he had just received from Colonel Stone's basecamp on the surface of Talia II again.

"That bad, huh?" his copilot, Jager, asked.

Farrell looked up from the report. "The *Vanguard* is lost, and Colonel Stone's unit on the surface is under attack by the same creatures that took her out."

"Yeah, that's pretty bad." Jager frowned. They had just finished a flyby of the *Vanguard* before they had received the colonel's new message. What they saw confirmed the colonel's message.

The *Vanguard* had risen out of the planet's orbit and retreated beyond the range of its gravitational pull, but her systems had been shut down. She was hung in space like a giant grave marker. Farrell couldn't think of any other way to describe her. The once powerful and noble ship's hull was now spotted with breaches from what appeared to be internal explosions, and with her systems shut down, she was dark and as dead as a human corpse. Farrell didn't dare try to board her. Captain Merrick had been a telemechanic, and Farrell knew he would have prepped the great ship for an easy start up for anyone with the proper codes to initiate it so she could be recovered. Even though the dropship's A.Is showed the *Vanguard* to be empty of life, Farrell didn't trust them. Besides, it would take a lot more people than just himself, Jager, and Harrison and Lumley aboard the other dropship to bring the *Vanguard* back to life and hold her against the enemy they were dealing with. The creatures that both Captain Merrick and Colonel Stone talked about in their messages were psycho-porters of the highest order. Not even bringing the *Vanguard*'s shields online would keep the creatures from getting aboard her again if they wanted to.

Farrell's fingers danced over the controls of the dropship, setting a course for a return to Talia II.

"I guess we're going back to the basecamp down there," Jager said.

Nodding, Farrell answered, "We're likely their only hope, Jager, and they're ours too. If we want the *Vanguard* back, we're going to need their guns and numbers."

Farrell activated the dropship's comm. "Lumley, I want you to follow us in, guns hot. Make sure Harrison breaks open the weapons locker over there. If those things try to teleport in and board you, you're going to want him armed."

Jager laughed, patting the shotgun that leaned against his copilot seat. "I think we're as ready as we can be over here," he added over the comm.

Harrison's laughter echoed in the dropship's pilot compartment. "Jager, you couldn't hit the board side of a barn man. Farrell is screwed if they decide to board and come after y'all."

"That nerd Lumley isn't any better than I am," Jager argued.

"Hey now!" Farrell and Jager heard Lumley protest.

"They may not even know we're here," Harrison pointed out.

"Don't count on that," Farrell countered him. "We've no idea how those things knew about the *Vanguard* to board her. They could very well be aware of us too."

Harrison and Lumley were silent.

"Let's just get this done," Farrell said and kicked the dropship's engine into overdrive. It spun away from the course that had taken it in for a look at the *Vanguard* and plummeted towards the surface of Talia II. Harrison's dropship followed after it.

The flight down was a bumpy one. Turbulence rocked the dropship, jarring Farrell and Jager about in their seats. Flames erupted over the dropship's hull, raging with a vicious fury then ceased to be as the dropship broke through and leveled out inside the atmosphere of Talia II.

Farrell slowed the dropship to get a reading on the basecamp's location in relation to where they were. The basecamp was about one hundred and fifty miles south of them. He kicked the engines into gear again, and the dropship soared across the night sky like she was an assault fighter. The dropships were heavily armored and were not without teeth. They hadn't been built for combat with other ships, but they were plenty tough enough to offer air support to ground troops that were in trouble. Farrell didn't really know what to expect at the basecamp Colonel Stone and her men had set up, but there was no way in Hades he was going to take the two dropships in on a slow approach. He figured as soon as the creatures saw them coming in that the things would start teleporting aboard them. Just one of the creatures might be enough to take them out of the sky. A missed shot inside the dropship or one of the creatures sinking its claws into a critical system would certainly do just that. No, his plan was to hit the things fast and hit them hard.

As the dropship raced towards the basecamp, Farrell called up a visual image of the camp, zooming in through the sensors' low-light mode. The image that came into being on his console made him want to be sick. There were bodies everywhere, the crumpled corpses of the creatures and the men and women of Colonel

Stone's unit too. Scattered bursts of gunfire blazed, but they were far apart and few in number. Neither of the two APCs' cannons was firing, Farrell realized. He didn't know if they had been damaged or if the creatures had made it inside the APCs to take out the troopers within them. The creatures were more nightmarish than he imagined. They ranged in size from seven to nine feet tall, all muscle, hair, and wings as they blinked into and out of existence around the camp. The dropship's sensor couldn't get a hard lock on just how many of the things there were, but the computer's best guess estimated the number of the creatures to be in the hundreds.

"Guns hot and targeting system online!" Jager informed him.

Jager had opted to let the dropship's computer do the targeting of the creatures. Given their number and constantly changing locations, Farrell thought that was a wise move.

"Colonel Stone!" Farrell shouted over the channel to the base he had opened. "This is Dropship Alpha and Beta, we're coming in hot."

That was all the warning he could give Stone, and Farrell hoped it was enough. The dropships would be firing directly into the camp. Their computers were designed for such close in firing, but that didn't mean they were perfect. Nothing was. There was always a chance that some of Stone's men would be caught in the Hell that were about to rain onto the bats.

"Light 'em up!" Farrell ordered, bringing the dropship in for a pass over the basecamp. Harrison, piloting Dropship Beta, followed him in.

The twin forward auto-cannons of each of the two dropships spun, hosing the basecamp with high-velocity rounds that streaked through the night like miniature flashes of rapid lightning. The bat creatures the dropships' computers targeted were ripped apart beneath the fury of the barrage. Some of the things took so many rounds their bodies were reduced to little more than splatters of gore. Others, trying to dodge, lost arms or legs as the rounds blew their limbs from their bodies. Most of the bats that didn't perish in those first couple of seconds began to bug out, vanishing into nothingness as they teleported away, to where? Only God knew.

"Pull up!" Jager cried as a bat creature teleported directly into the dropship's path. Farrell saw the twisted snarling lips of the monster as he stared at it through the dropship's forward window. The thing had no eyes. It had the sockets on its face that should have held them, but they were overgrown with a thick layer of gray flesh. The creature's body was covered in a coarse, black hair. Flapping its wings, the creature held its position, defiantly, in the air in front of the dropship until the ship struck it. Farrell didn't feel the impact. The dropship was built to withstand much more than an impact with something that was merely flesh and bone. The creature's guts and blood splashed over the dropship's window, staining it black. Farrell felt sick but managed to hold himself together. The forward window was drenched in black, but that didn't matter. He had been flying by the ship's sensors, not visually through the window anyway.

"Frag me!" Jager yelped. "That thing was crazy!"

"Hold on!" Farrell ordered as the dropship came to the end of its strafing run over the camp and he jerked its controls, causing the ship to break hard to the right. Farrell kept the ship clear of the tall trees that lined the perimeter of the camp and began to pull up. As he did so, he sensed that something was behind him. He wasn't gifted and had no psionic ability. It was just that creepy feeling one got when something was about to go horribly wrong.

The bat creature popped into existence inside the dropship behind the two pilot seats and came lunging at Jager. To his credit, Jager sprang from his seat to meet it, sweeping up his shotgun from the floor into his hands as he went. Jager had the foresight to have a round already chambered in the weapon. He brought the shotgun's barrel up at the monster hissing and snarling as its clawed hands reached out at him.

Farrell heard the shotgun's thunderous blast as Jager got a shot off at the monster. The slug the shotgun spat missed its intended target to go ricocheting around the pilot's compartment.

"Frag!" Farrell cursed as the slug pinged against the dropship's wall next to him before slamming into the forward window. The window cracked but held. Farrell thanked God that it had.

Lumley's voice rang out over the comm. screaming, "Harrison is dead! We're going down!"

Farrell knew that the same thing that was happening behind had to have happened on Dropship Beta. One of the creatures had teleported aboard and taken Harrison out. Lumley was still alive, for the moment, but from what he was saying, he wouldn't be long. The creature that had killed Harrison had likely damaged Dropship Beta's controls or some other critical system. Farrell managed to get his own dropship what he hoped was a safe distance from the raging battle of Colonel Stone's basecamp, though in truth, he didn't know there was such a thing. The creatures had, after all, teleported from the planet's surface all the way to the *Vanguard* somehow.

Whipping his head around to take a look at the fight going on behind his pilot seat, Farrell saw Jager blow the bat creature's leg from underneath it. The blast from Jager's shotgun pulped the thing's right knee, severing the leg below it from the thing's body. The bat creature flopped to the floor, still reaching for Jager. One of its clawed hands caught Jager by his groin, slashing his thighs in the process. Red blossomed on Jager's crouch, seeping through the cloth of his pants as blood ran along his legs in streaming rivers. Jager's howl was like that of dying cat's. The bat creature used its hold on Jager to drag him closer to it. Jager was still fighting despite his pain. He rammed the barrel of the shotgun outward, shoving it into the bat creature's open mouth. The shotgun thundered again as the bat creature's head exploded in a shower of brain matter, bone fragments, and black blood. Jager slumped to the dropship's floor next to the creature's headless corpse.

A pool of blood was forming around Jager where he sat as Farrell set the dropship to hold its position and leaped from his seat, rushing to Jager's side.

Tears were streaming over Jager's cheeks and his skin was a deathly shade of pale.

"I got him, man," Jager croaked proudly. "I got the bastard."

"Yes, you did," Farrell said, feigning a smile, as he attempted to comfort Jager.

"Get 'em all," Jager told him and then died in Farrell's arms. Jager's wounds had been so severe that he had bled out already.

"I will, buddy," Farrell promised. "I will."

****

Noel came awake with a jolt. Her eyes were wild as they took in the sight of Barnes above her. The precog was well and full gone. Blood leaked from his nose, ears, and eyes. Whatever he had seen in the future had been too much for him. Noel's own mind had suppressed the vision of she had shared with Barnes in his final moments, or it would have been the same for her. She had knowledge that she had protected herself by burying the images that cooked Barnes' mind but, thankfully, no knowledge of what they were. Her head jerked about as she took in surroundings, thankful for the cold feel of Alpha I's metal floor beneath her palms.

Sergeant Lesniak and the unit's scout, Brasiliat, shared the APC's rear compartment with her. They were bruised, battered, covered in the midnight-black blood of the bat creatures, and fresh from battle. Noel could sense the minds of Colonel Stone and the APC's driver, McGregor, in the front of the vehicle. The sounds of the battle outside its armored walls had changed. There was very little gunfire now. The bulk of the noise outside was the screeching, violent cries of the bat creatures. Then it hit her that if Lesniak and Brasiliat had retreated inside Alpha I, the battle was surely lost or soon would be.

"Dropships inbound!" she heard Colonel Stone shout from the forward compartment.

Then the APC seemed to shake as a cacophony of fire rained onto the battle outside Alpha I's armored walls. The sound of the dropships' autocannons was like something straight out of Hell. The screeches and shrieks of the bat creatures turned from ones of violence to stark terror and pain. McGregor was whooping in triumph as the bats outside died by the hundreds.

Noel couldn't help herself. She was terrified and *needed* to see what was happening. She made contact with Colonel Stone's mind every so subtly, making sure that Stone was unaware of her mental presence. Through Stone's eyes, Noel watched the bats being driven back, their ranks gutted by the fire of the two dropships. She felt the colonel's hope swelling and the pleasure the colonel took in the death of so many of the bats. It was a justified vengeance to Stone. Through Alpha I's forward window, Stone looked out to see the two dropships as they swept over the APC and past it. Then suddenly, one of the dropships wobbled in the sky. It veered off-course, spinning through the air. The dropship vanished from sight as it went down among the distant trees. The explosion that followed lit up the night. She felt Stone's hope crumbling and twisting into a bitter resentment at the hand fate appeared to be dealing her. The other dropship kept its course though. It completed its run and cleared the field of battle, streaking away in the night sky. Stone was counting the seconds in her mind as Noel listened in. The colonel was waiting on the surviving dropship to return for a second run. It didn't. Stone let loose a litany of curses that would have made the foulest of spacers blush as Noel withdrew from her mind.

Noel's consciousness returned to her own body to find the sergeant, Lesniak, kneeling over her.

"Are you okay?" the big, scarred man was asking her in a gentle voice.

Noel didn't know how to answer him. Barnes' vision of the future was locked away in the recesses of her thoughts, burning there, and demanding to be viewed though she didn't dare do so. And she had felt Colonel Stone's fear as one dropship died and the other didn't return. She understood what that meant for them all in the basecamp. She glanced over at Barnes' limp form and finally said, "I'm not dead…yet."

The big sergeant nodded his understanding and stood up to give her some space as Colonel Stone entered the rear compartment.

"One of the dropships is down and the other is gone," Colonel Stone told them all.

"Figured that was what the explosion out there was," Brasiliat commented. The scout had been standing like he was in some sort of trance. His attention focused on Alpha I's walls. The arrival of the dropships had caused him to lose focus though. "The bats likely got aboard it. Doubt there was any other way they could have taken it out."

"Frag!" Lesniak roared.

"We have to get out here, Colonel," Brasiliat urged. "I'm surprised the bats haven't targeted our two APCs more already."

Colonel Stone nodded. "Agreed, we've got no choice but to cut our losses and run. Brasiliat, get back to keeping making sure those creatures don't get in here. Lesniak, watch after Noel. I'll be up front with McGregor."

With that, Colonel Stone turned on her heel and re-entered the driver's compartment. Almost as an afterthought, she called back at them, "And I suggest you all strap in or at least find something to hold onto."

"You heard the lady," Lesniak said, roughly helping Noel to her feet. "You better get strapped in."

Noel took a seat, far from where Lesniak was strapping in Barnes' body so that it wouldn't go bouncing about the compartment when things hit the fan. She clicked the seat's safety harness tight around her.

"What about you?" Noel asked, noticing Lesniak remained on his feet.

"Don't you worry about me," Lesniak said, "I've been through stuff a lot rough than this. Besides, I'm telekinetic."

"I still think…" Noel started, but Brasiliat cut her off.

"Let the big man do his job," the scout ordered her. "Someone has to be ready to deal with any bats that might get in here if I can't keep them out. Keeping your mouth shut so I can focus wouldn't hurt either."

Brasiliat had strapped himself in a seat across from where she sat. She watched as he settled into the trance like he had been in when she woke up once more. Noel didn't have a clue how the scout was going to keep the bats out. Not really. She figured it had something to do with psionically blocking the pathways into the vehicle though, even if she didn't understand how the type of gift Brasiliat possessed worked.

Noel heard Alpha I's engine rev to life and the APC started moving.

****

McGregor drove the Alpha I through the carnage that littered the basecamp. The huge wheels of the vehicle crushed the corpses of bat creatures and dead soldiers alike as it rolled out. The APC picked up speed as it went. Every so often, one of the less intelligent bat creatures would pop into existence in its path, trying to attack the vehicle's forward window. McGregor drove straight through them, smashing their bodies against the front of the APOC or running them over. Alpha I's forward window was designed to withstand the blast of an RPG, so the odds of the bats breaking through it were slim. With the roof-mounted auto-cannon out of commission, Alpha I had no weapons to strike at the bats with, so McGregor kept the acceleration pedal floored. The driver of Alpha II appeared to be having a tough time keeping up with him but was managing to do so, if barely, thus far.

As McGregor drove, Colonel Stone was busy on its comm., attempting to contact the remaining dropship which she very much hoped was still out there somewhere and functional.

"This is Alpha I to Dropship Alpha!" Colonel Stone shouted over the channel she had opened. "Answer me, frag it! That's an order!"

On her third attempt, she finally got a reply.

"This is Dropship Alpha, Alpha I," the voice of Lieutenant Farrell crackled over the channel.

"Farrell!" Colonel Stone exclaimed. "Thank God!"

"I wouldn't thank him just yet, ma'am," Farrell said, "Dropship Beta is down, and we were boarded by one of those bat creatures. My copilot, Jager, is dead. I'm flying alone up here."

"Where is that exactly?" Colonel Stone demanded.

"I'm about fifty miles north of your position," Farrell answered. "I have you on sensors, ma'am."

"Good," Colonel Stone commented. "As I am sure you can see, we're on the move. Despite your assistance, basecamp was lost."

"I'm sorry to hear that, ma'am," Farrell replied.

"We need a place to regroup…somewhere that we can defend," Colonel Stone said.

"I don't think there is one on this planet, Colonel," Farrell sighed. "The *Vanguard* is still in orbit though. Captain Merrick killed her life support and vented her atmosphere to drive the bats that had boarded her out. She's just waiting up there and very likely prepped to be brought online again with just a few commands. Captain Merrick sent me the codes we'd need for that before—"

"Understood," Colonel Stone interrupted to save Farrell from talking about Captain Merrick's death aloud. The captain's death was a blow them all, even those who didn't know him personally like she had. "That's the plan then. Still, we need a spot where we can come aboard. Somewhere open where we can better deal with any bats that try to stop us."

"There's a large clearing about twenty miles north of your current position. I am sending you the coordinates for it now," Farrell told her.

Colonel Stone watched the data as it downloaded to her screen. "Got them, Lieutenant. We'll meet you there. Be ready."

"Yes, ma'am," Farrell answered. "Dropship Alpha, out."

"McGregor," Colonel Stone turned her head towards where he fought with the APC's steering wheel in the driver's seat, navigating the heavy vehicle through the forest as best he could.

"I got the coordinate too, Colonel," McGregor told her. "Doing my best. I promise."

"Roger that," Colonel Stone barked as she shifted in her seat to look into the APC's rear compartment. "Sergeant Lesniak! Brasiliat! We've established contact with Dropship Alpha. We'll be meeting up with in a large clearing to the north. Be ready!"

****

Alpha II's normal driver was long dead. Private Peter Higgins sat in its driver's seat as he jerked the heavy vehicle's steering wheel hard to left, dodging yet another tree as he tried to keep up with Alpha I. Whoever was driving Alpha I was either the best driver Higgins had ever seen or an utter madman with no regard for his own safety. The chances he took with such hard turns at the speed the two APCs were moving at were insane. Only the grace of God had kept Higgins from losing control of Alpha II as he tried to keep up with the maniac.

Thacker, Mckinney, and Brooks were in Alpha II's rear compartment. They were the only survivors who had made it into the APC with him after the bats had ravaged the vehicle's interior during the battle at the basecamp. Red and black smears of mixed human and bat blood stained the vehicle's walls and floor, though the four of them had been able to toss out all the corpses they had found inside the APC before Colonel Stone had ordered them to roll out.

"Bat!" Higgins heard Mckinney shout from the rear compartment as another of the things teleported into it. The bat creature's sharp shriek almost made Higgins' lose control of his bladder. Its cry was followed by the sound of gunfire as Mckinney and the others in the rear opened fire on the monster. Bullets pinged around in the APC's rear compartment as at least of the men missed the monster. Someone screamed. Another voice cried out in pure agony to the point of sounding almost inhuman. Then it was all over.

"We got the bastard!" Higgins heard Thacker shout at him. "Mckinney is dead though. The bat tore his face off!"

"Brooks?" Higgins asked.

"Here," the private said in grunt that sounded like it came through gritted teeth. "Caught a ricochet in my side. Bleeding pretty bad, but I am hanging in there!"

"Great," Higgins muttered to himself and thought, *If those idiots in the rear can't keep the bats out, we're all freaking dead, even if I can keep up with the psycho in front of me.*

"Bat!" he heard Thacker shout again, but this time, there was no shrieking cry or roar of gunfire. Instead, Higgins heard a sharp hissing noise from directly beside him. He turned his head to glance to his right in the direction of the seat next to him. The bat had teleported into it. It lunged over at him, its lips twisted in a snarl that showed the razor-like teeth within its mouth, still smeared red with the blood of the human it had killed.

"Help!" Higgins cried out, instinctively going for the pistol holster on his hip. The bat was too close though. Its teeth sunk into the soft flesh of his throat. Higgins' blood sprayed over Alpha II's forward window. With no one guiding the course of the heavy APC at such a high speed, the vehicle veered sideways. It took out several trees, like a tank plowing through them, before one of the trees finally hit it at an angle that upended the vehicle. The APC flipped upwards and then over to go sliding through the forest on its roof. Seconds later, it exploded in a ball of blossoming fire that reached upwards towards the night sky as the ammo it carried inside its auto-cannon was detonated by the impact of the crash.

****

McGregor saw Alpha II swerving about wildly behind Alpha I. He watched helplessly as the other APC crashed into one tree after another, finally striking one that flipped it over onto its roof. Alpha II skidded along the forest floor before it blew. McGregor jerked his eyes away from the blinding light of the exploding APC on the screen that showed the view what lay behind Alpha I.

"We've lost Alpha II!" he told Colonel Stone.

"Frag it!" Colonel Stone smashed a balled-up fist in the wall next to her seat beside him.

McGregor didn't bother to ask if he should turn around to check for survivors. If he did, there wouldn't be any aboard Alpha I either. The bat creatures would surely pin them down and kill them all. He kept his focus on the forest ahead of the heavy vehicle he drove.

"How close are we to the clearing?" Colonel Stone shouted at him.

"Should be coming up any time now, ma'am," McGregor told her.

Alpha I burst from the trees into the wide clearing that Dropship Alpha had directed them to. He slammed on the brakes, sending the heavy APC sliding sideways deeper into it. Bat creatures were teleporting into the clearing before the APC had even come to a complete stop. The things appeared all around the heavy vehicle and on top of it. Sparks flew as their claws slashed against its armor.

Dropship Alpha came sweeping into view over the clearing, its auto-cannons blazing. The streams of fire from them chewed up bat flesh as the dropship's pilot, Farrell, hosed the bat creatures near Alpha I. Dozens up dozens of the bat creatures died beneath the barrage from the dropship, their bodies being mangled into little more than a mess of gore that stained the APC's armor and the grass around it. The dropship kept firing as came in for a landing as close Alpha I as it could safely touchdown.

"Time to move!" Colonel Stone ordered McGregor, tossing him a rifle.

McGregor caught it and sprang from his seat after the colonel as she raced into the APC's rear compartment and the wide, side door there. Sergeant Lesniak, Brasiliat, who was the unit's scout, and the telepath, Noel, awaited them there.

"Brasiliat!" Colonel Stone yelled. "Take Noel and get on over there. I want you to keep those things from getting aboard Alpha I!"

"Wha...?" Noel started, but then was gone as Brasiliat thrust an arm about her waist, pulling her close to him, and the pair blinked out of existence, leaving only empty space where they had once been.

"What about him?" the big sergeant, Lesniak, shouted, gesturing at Barnes who still sat, braindead on one of Alpha I's rear seats. "We can't just leave him here."

Colonel Stone took a quick step towards the precog, pressing the barrel of her pistol to Barnes' forehead. The precog's limp body jerked as the shot from Colonel Stone's pistol echoed inside the rear compartment and splattered whatever was left of Barnes' brains onto the wall behind where he sat. His corpse slid from the seat he was sitting in to thump to the floor of the APC.

Lesniak looked like he was going to make a move against Colonel Stone, but she stopped him by shouting, "It's better than what the bats would have done to him, and you know it, Sergeant!"

The sergeant gave a grunt of understanding as he nodded coldly at Colonel Stone.

Colonel Stone whipped around him as McGregor readied the rifle she had given him.

"Get that blasted door open, McGregor!" Colonel Stone ordered him. "We need to get moving!"

McGregor punched the control code that opened the APC's side door into the keypad next to it. As the door slid open, two of the bat creatures were waiting on them. McGregor knew that Lesniak was a telekinetic, but the big sergeant still surprised him with what he did. Lesniak's right hand flew up in the direction of the two bats, and an invisible force crushed their bodies before McGregor's eyes. Then Colonel Stone's hand was on his back, shoving McGregor out of the APC into the clearing. McGregor stumbled from the APC as Colonel Stone and the big sergeant hopped out after him. He still trying to recover and find his balance as the two of them started shooting. The bat creatures were everywhere. One of the monsters leaped from the top of the APC at them, only to be met with a blast from Lesniak's weapon that caused its skull to explode like an overripe melon. The thing's headless corpse crashed to the forest floor in front of where Lesniak stood.

"Move!" Colonel Stone yelled at him as she ran by, heading for the open side door of Dropship Alpha. Brasiliat was standing in the doorway, his pistols spitting rapid death in the bats who were foolish enough to approach it.

One of the bat creatures came at McGregor as he ran after Colonel Stone towards the dropship. Blasting at the monster with his rifle, he put a burst of rounds into the thing's chest that sent it reeling backwards away from him.

Colonel Stone reached the open door of the dropship, shoving Brasiliat further inside it. "Keep your focus on stopping those things from teleporting in here! I've got the door!" she screamed at the scout.

McGregor reached the doorway, diving past Colonel Stone into the dropship as she covered him. He looked out into the clearing to see Lesniak grappling with a trio of the bat creatures that clung to him. The big sergeant almost seemed to glow. McGregor saw that it wasn't Lesniak that was glowing but the telekinetic field that shimmered around his body, protecting him from the claws and teeth that tried to tear at him. One of the bat creatures took flight, springing from the big sergeant's back into the air. Its wings flapped in a mad panic as its hands clawed at its own throat. McGregor knew it was the doing of the big sergeant. He had seen people telekinetically choked before. The other two creatures clinging to Lesniak grew even more furious in their efforts to get at him. Bullets pinged off that glowing shield around Lesniak as Colonel Stone opened fire on him. The two bat creatures weren't protected from her rounds like the big sergeant was. Her rounds ripped into them. Then Lesniak was free of the things. His pace picked up as he continued to run towards Dropship Alpha's open door.

"McGregor!" Colonel Stone yelled. "Help him!"

The APC driver's rifle clattered to the dropship's floor at his feet and let go of the weapon, and he rushed forward to take Lesniak's hand, tugging him up and through the doorway. Colonel Stone threw herself from the path the door that slid into place as soon as Lesniak was inside.

McGregor heard someone groaning and whipped his head around in the direction that sound came from. Brasiliat was sitting on the dropship's floor, staring at its ceiling. The scout's face was terribly contorted in pain, his hands clutching the sides of his head. The smallest trickles of blood ran from the corners of his eyes.

Colonel Stone rushed to the scout and kneeled next to him. "Come on, man! You can do this! You kept those things out of the APC."

"Not very many...tried for APC," Brasiliat grunted. "All of them...want in here."

"Get us airborne!" Sergeant Lesniak screamed at Dropship Alpha's pilot, Farrell.

"Trust me, I'm trying," Farrell shouted in reply. "Those things are all over the hull!"

McGregor could hear the dropship's engines straining against the weight and pull of the bat creatures. Hundreds of them had teleported onto the ship's exterior since Brasiliat was still managing to keep them from truly getting inside its hull. Even more of them, around it on the ground, had taken hold of the ship, wedging their claws into its armor, trying to hold it in place. McGregor knew the things were far stronger than humans, but to see that strength displayed in such a manner left him utterly amazed and terrified at once.

"I'll get them off the hull," Lesniak roared. He pressed his clenched fists to his temples and closed his eyes. The big sergeant huffed like a weight lifter straining. In the moment that followed, the bat creatures were flung from the top of the dropship and it shot like a bullet, upwards, into the night sky.

"Yeah!" McGregor heard the pilot shouting in victory. "That's the bloody ticket that is!"

Brasiliat slumped forward into Colonel Stone's arms, looking relieved. Colonel Stone held him close, looking down at his exhausted face.

"Most of them have stopped, ma'am," Brasiliat told her. "Only a few are still trying to board us."

"Can you keep them out?" Colonel Stone asked with grave concern in her voice. The psycho-porter was their only hope at keeping the bat creatures from merely appearing inside the dropship, all claws and fury.

Brasiliat nodded weakly. "For now…"

"Why did they stop?" McGregor asked, stunned by the sound of his own voice.

"Could be what the big guy did to them," Farrell shouted into the rear compartment of the dropship from where he sat in the pilot seat. "He blew those mothers apart, man. Never seen anything like it."

Only then did McGregor notice that Lesniak had collapsed to the dropship's floor. Noel was staring at him in horror. Lesniak lay in a pool of his own blood. Red leaked from his ears, nose, and the side of his mouth. His eyes bulged in their sockets, nearly blown out of his skull by whatever pressure had been inside it from the last use of his power.

McGregor wanted to help him, but his body wouldn't move. He was lost in shock. McGregor could only watch as Noel squatted beside the big sergeant, pressing her fingertips to his neck. "It's not just his brain," she said as she confirmed it for herself, "his body is dead too. The strain of whatever he did to those bats on and around the ship killed him."

"God have mercy on him," McGregor stammered, realizing he could move again, and crossed himself.

"Five," McGregor heard Colonel Stone say where she sat still cradling Brasiliat. "Only five left."

McGregor knew what she meant. Of the entire unit dispatched to Talia II, including the crew of the *Vanguard,* the five of them aboard the dropship were all that was left alive.

****

"We're approaching the *Vanguard* now, Colonel Stone," Farrell said.

"Can you open its hangar doors remotely?" Colonel Stone asked.

Farrell snorted. "I don't think that'll be a problem, ma'am. The hangar is blown to Hell and back. I can take us straight in."

"Do it," Colonel Stone ordered.

Dropship Alpha eased itself into the larger ship's hangar bay, or rather the remnants of it. Dropship Alpha's landing gear clanged against the metal of the bay's floor so loudly it could be heard inside it as Farrell landed.

Colonel Stone had passed over the care of Brasiliat to Noel. It was the telepath who sat on the floor holding him now. As a telepath, Noel could add her mental strength to the scout's. Even so, it looked doubtful that Brasiliat would be able to keep the bat creatures out much longer. The exchange had left Colonel Stone free to do what needed to be done though. She had moved into the forward section of Dropship Alpha and taken its copilot seat.

"Farrell, can this dropship access the *Vanguard*'s systems?" Colonel Stone asked.

"In a limited fashion, I suppose." Farrell shrugged. "Why?"

"You said Captain Merrick sent you the command codes to bring the *Vanguard*'s primary systems online again. He sent me a copy of them as well. Bringing them online from here and getting some integrity shields active in this bay would be a fragging lot easier than trying to suit up in environmental gear and trying to make it to the bridge."

"I hear what you're saying, ma'am." Farrell nodded. "Won't hurt to try. If Captain Merrick were with us…"

"He could do it with just a thought," Colonel Stone finished the pilot's sentence. "He's not though, is he?"

"No, ma'am," Farrell answered sadly.

"So we best get at it." Colonel Stone thumped a fist against the dropship's controls. "Brasiliat could lose his fight against those things at any moment. I, for one, would rather fight them in the *Vanguard*'s corridors rather than in the confined space of this dropship."

"Roger that, ma'am." Farrell shot her a wry grin as he leaned over the dropship's controls and went to work at establishing an interface between them and the *Vanguard*'s main computer. Farrell suddenly stopped and looked over at Colonel Stone. "Tell me, ma'am, do we have a plan for what we're going to do after we get the *Vanguard*'s system online?"

"We're going to get the hell out of this system," Colonel Stone told him bluntly.

****

The *Vanguard*'s A.I., Val, was unrecoverable. All the changes made by Captain Merrick to the ship's system in such haste, combined with the physical damage to the ship from the bat creatures' attack on it, had essentially destroyed the A.I. Given time, Val could be restored and brought online again, but time was something that none of them had. Colonel Stone knew they could fly the ship without Val's aid…at least far enough to escape the range of the bat creatures' ability to reach them. She wanted very badly to ask Brasiliat just how that the range of that ability might extend, but Brasiliat was barely hanging on. His own strength was gone. Only Noel's kept him hanging on as the telepath gave the psycho-porter all she could of her own willpower and mind to help him keep the bat creatures at bay.

Farrell let out a whoop as the *Vanguard*'s system came online. "We did it!" he shouted.

"Great." Colonel Stone did her best to smile, though she knew just how little it would matter if they didn't reach the ship's bridge before the bat creatures got onboard. Farrell had already confirmed for her that tapping into the ship's nav. system and helm was impossible from the dropship. Those systems were simply too complex to be manipulated through the limited interface the dropship could handle. "Get some integrity shields up to seal up this hangar and restore atmosphere to it. We need to get moving."

"Yes, ma'am." Farrell nodded.

Colonel Stone left her seat, entering the rear of the dropship. McGregor had covered Sergeant Lesniak's body with a blanket taken from one of the dropship's emergency caches. The sergeant's blood had soaked through the blanket, staining it red. Colonel Stone felt pain as she paused to stare at Lesniak's covered corpse. She hadn't known the big man especially well, but she had seen enough of his action to know that he had been a professional soldier, through and through. He kept fighting right up until the end, doing what he could to give the rest of them a chance. The loss of a man like him hit her hard. So many had died in the last day. Men and women who had entrusted their lives to her and now had left their loved ones to mourn when news of their deaths reached home. Guilt tore at her soul, but the anger she felt towards the bats was stronger.

"McGregor!" she shouted at the former APC driver. "Gear up. We've got to reach the bridge. It's up to us now."

McGregor looked like he wanted to protest. She knew he didn't have a lot of combat experience outside of armored vehicles. Colonel Stone didn't blame him for being scared. None of them would be human if they didn't feel at least some fear given the circumstances.

"What about them?" McGregor asked, gesturing towards the telepath who still sat clutching Brasiliat to her.

"Brasiliat is in no shape to be moved. Doing so would likely be the end of whatever shield he's holding up to keep the bats out. Farrell will stay here with them," Colonel Stone said.

"I will?" Farrell asked from behind as he stood in the doorway to that led into the forward compartment of the dropship.

Colonel Stone nodded. "Watch over those two. Keep them safe, Farrell. If you haven't heard back from us in two hours, take this dropship out into space again and get as far from Talia II as you can. The *Seeder* isn't that far behind us. You might just have enough power left to keep this dropship's life support going until it does. Tell them about the planet, Farrell, and make sure they stay the hell away from it."

"Understood," Farrell answered her, frowning. "Two hours then."

McGregor had somehow managed to find a shotgun and the rounds for it one of the dropship's emergency caches. He had strapped next magazines for the weapon onto his belt. Colonel Stone spotted a pair of grenades dangling from the driver's belt as well. She hoped it wouldn't get rough enough for them to have to be used.

"Ready when you are, ma'am," McGregor said, though he clearly wasn't.

"The shields are up, and atmosphere has been restored to the hangar," Farrell said. "Good luck out there."

Colonel Stone glanced at McGregor and then headed for the dropship's rear door. "Come on then," she ordered him.

The dropship's exit ramp clanged onto the metal floor of the hangar as she led McGregor down it. "Don't suppose you know the shortest route to the bridge, do you?"

McGregor laughed, maybe to cover the fear he was feeling. "Not a clue," he admitted.

The dropship's ramp raised up to close itself after they were clear of it. Colonel Stone tapped her comm. "Farrell, can you direct us which way to go?"

"Head for the lift at the far end of the hangar. It's undamaged and should at least get you up to the next deck, and then we'll take from there as it goes."

****

Once inside the lift, Colonel Stone double-checked the rifle she had snagged from the dropship, making sure it was ready for action. She felt McGregor watching her. "What is it?" she asked.

"Nothing," McGregor said, turning his gaze away from her. "I was just thinking."

"About what?" Colonel Stone asked.

"That you're pretty hot for a colonel, ma'am." McGregor grinned.

All the tension pent up within her broke as Colonel Stone burst into laughter. It was good to laugh. There had been so much darkness since the *Vanguard* had entered the Talia system and Val had awoken them all from stasis.

"For a colonel, huh?" she teased him.

"Yep," McGregor assured her. "I mean, I like my women tough enough to handle themselves, but a full-fledged colonel who could kick my butt? Well, that's a bit much I think."

Before Colonel Stone could reply, the lift reached its destination, and with a sharp ping, its doors swooshed open. She was in the corridor outside it first, sweeping the area with the barrel of her rifle, finger ready on the weapon's trigger. She let out a sigh of relief as she there weren't any of the bat creatures, other than scattered corpses along the corridor floor, around. There were bodies everywhere through the *Vanguard* as she and McGregor made their way towards the bridge. The whole ship must have been turned into a warzone before Captain Merrick had ended it all. Some areas the bodies were thicker than others, and it was clear that in those areas, the fighting had been heavy.

Colonel Stone realized that McGregor had stopped behind her. She turned to see him staring at the body of a young woman. The woman's hand clutched a piece of ragged piping. From the bat corpse that lay on top of her, it had been enough to get her vengeance on the monster that had killed her. Its head was caved in from what looked to be repeated blows to the top of its skull. The woman's throat was torn out, a mess of jagged, shredded flesh, but in her adrenaline heightened last moments, she had gotten the job of dragging the bat into the next life with her done.

McGregor's eyes glistened with tears that refused to fall. He must have noticed her watching him because he glanced her way and said, "This is all such a nightmare."

"Let's just make sure it's one we wake up from," Colonel Stone said. "We can't help her. We can't help any of them, but we can frag well make sure we don't end up like them."

"Right," McGregor said weakly, though he gave her a sharp nod. "Lead on, Colonel."

The comm. on Colonel Stone's helmet crackled. Farrell's voice came over it. "Colonel Stone, I'm picking up two lifeforms near your current position. They're weak but definitely there."

"Bats?" Colonel Stone asked, holding up a hand at McGregor so he wouldn't interrupt what Farrell was telling her.

"I don't think so, Colonel, but I can't be sure. Both lifeforms are coming from the medical area to your left," Farrell said.

"We'll check it out," Colonel Stone told the pilot. They didn't really have the time to waste. Every second that went by was one more that Brasiliat had to strain to keep the bats from teleporting onto the *Vanguard*. Truth be told, she would have thought Brasiliat would have caved-in from the stress he was under already. He was only one man, and the number of bats seemed limitless. She had no idea how he was doing what he was doing. Brasiliat had once told her that teleporting, or blinking as he liked to call it, was more like an art form than a science. It was about an instinctive feel for the pathways and dimensions around you. A good psycho-porter could not only open them but bend them as well or shift them about. If it had been merely like holding a door closed, surely his one mind against so many wouldn't have had a chance much less been able to keep the bat creatures at bay as long as he already had. If they lived through this mess, she hoped to have a drink with the scout and ask him about it. Of course, living through the mess was the tricky part. Regardless of whatever Brasiliat was doing to keep the bat creatures out, he couldn't do it forever, and each passing second that ticked by was priceless. Still, if the lifeforms were bat creatures, it was better to deal with the monsters now rather than take a chance at running into the things on *their* terms later.

"We need to go in there." Colonel Stone gestured at the medical bay with the barrel of her rifle.

"But I thought the bridge...?" McGregor started.

"It *is* our priority, but Farrell says there's something alive in there. Whether it's some of the bat creatures or survivors of the battle on this ship, we need to check it out," Colonel Stone explained.

"You're the boss." McGregor flashed another one of his roguish grins at her.

The door to the medical bay was sealed. Colonel Stone and McGregor took up positions facing each at its sides. Colonel Stone keyed in the code to open the door all except for the last digit and looked at McGregor. "You ready?"

"No," McGregor answered honestly.

"On three then…" Colonel Stone told him.

"One…two…three!" she shouted as she punched in the final number of the code and the door swished open. She was through it in a heartbeat, her rifle ready. A human hand shot out from her left flank as she rushed inside the medical bay. It grabbed the end of her rifle, jerking it downwards towards the floor.

"Colonel!" a voice screamed at her.

"Don't shoot!" another cried out.

Colonel Stone blinked as she took in the sight of Dr. Joseph Lumley and the mission's seventh gifted member looking at her in terror.

"Dr. Lumley!" Colonel Stone exclaimed, the surprise at seeing people still alive messing with her.

"Corporal Epiphany?" McGregor stuttered in disbelief as he entered the medical bay.

"McGregor!" Epiphany cried out as she saw him and ran to embrace him. "I knew someone would come for us!"

"What the hell happened here, Dr. Lumley?" Colonel Stone blurted out.

"The bat creatures attacked the ship in force. I had to kill one of the things myself." Lumley gestured at the withered body of something that might once have been one of the bats that lay on the floor of the medical bay not far away. The sight of the thing's body was utterly horrific. It wasn't just dead. It looked as if its very life had been sucked out of it and its body had been lying where it was for decades. Colonel Stone knew Dr. Lumley was a psycho-metabolist. Power over life and death were his to control. He could give it or take it away with nothing more than a touch and thought.

Colonel Stone shuddered and then shook herself to clear her head. "And you are?" she asked the woman.

"This is Corporal Rachel Epiphany, ma'am," McGregor told her. "She's a friend of mine from Boot, years ago. She's also one of the mission's gifted."

"Really?" Colonel Stone asked her doubt heavy in her voice. "Why don't I know you? I read all the files about the gifted who were assigned to his mission."

Epiphany giggled. "Well, that's just how my gift works, ma'am. It either keeps me out of danger or keeps me alive when the crap does hit the fan. Likely you don't remember me because if you had known I was onboard and what my gift was, you would have taken me planet side with you. If you'd done that, I wouldn't have been here to save Dr. Lumley or perhaps here at all of that matter."

"She's what you called *charmed*, ma'am." McGregor's smile was wide as he spoke. "Some argue that being *charmed* isn't a real gift at all but rather some kind of supernatural interference in the charmed person's life. Personally, I just think it's another gift like precognition. It works on its own terms and the charmed person can't control it. It just happens."

"Okay." Colonel Stone shrugged. "And I suppose you being a charmed also explains how the two of you survived Captain Merrick shutting down all the *Vanguard's* systems. The two you should have run out of air in here, not to mention been frozen to death by now."

"Exactly." Epiphany grinned. "Something went wrong with the control circuit in here and the captain couldn't kill the systems, only the power to them, and I suspect he had to pull off some impressive bypass routes to do even that. As you know, the medical bay had its own backup power supply for emergencies. All Dr. Lumley had to do was turn that on and we were good to go until you guys got here."

"And the bat?" McGregor asked.

"I showed up as the medical bay doors were closing and just barely got inside. I was hunting for a place to hide and the medical bay seemed as good as any. Everyone else in here was dead but Dr. Lumley. The bat was making a move at him, but I distracted it at just the right moment so that he got the upper hand," Epiphany said. "But I really don't ever want to see Dr. Lumley do what he did to the bat again."

"And trust me, I was blessed by her showing up when she did. She not only saved me from the bat, but it was her that reminded me about the backup power systems in here. Without her, I was so shaken up I might not have been in a state of mind to even remember they existed. Doing what I did to the bat takes a lot out of me," Dr. Lumley added.

"So where's the rest of the rescue party?" Epiphany moved passed McGregor to peep into the corridor beyond him.

"Sorry, Epiphany," McGregor said. "We're not a rescue party, and we're it."

"What?" Dr. Lumley rasped.

"Counting the two of you," Colonel Stone told them, "there are only seven living humans onboard this ship and none on the planet below."

"My God..." Lumley stumbled, retreating a step from the colonel as if she had struck him.

"Those things killed everyone else," McGregor chimed in. "We're trying to get to the bridge so we can use the *Vanguard* to get the hell out of this star system and away from those monsters."

"'Cool!" Epiphany bounced like an excited little girl. "Count me in!"

"I suppose that goes for me too," Dr. Lumley said. "I'd like a weapon though."

"We'll hit this deck's weapons locker on the way up," Colonel Stone assured the doctor. "But we need to get moving. The bats could board this ship again at any moment."

****

Farrell heard Noel scream from where he sat in the pilot compartment of Dropship Alpha. He leaped from his seat and darted into the rear compartment. Noel had let Brasiliat's body drop to the floor and now sat staring at it. As he approached, she looked up at him with tears in her eyes.

"He's dead," she said. "It was too much for him."

"I'm sorry," Farrell told her, not knowing what else to say. Then it hit him that Brasiliat had been the only thing keeping the bat creatures from boarding the *Vanguard*. "Frag!" he shouted as he left Noel alone where she sat and raced back to his pilot seat. He flipped open a channel to Colonel Stone.

"Colonel!" he yelled over the open channel. "Brasiliat is gone!"

"Gone?" Colonel Stone asked. "What do you mean gone?"

"He's dead, ma'am," Farrell informed her. "I guess the strain of keeping the bat creatures out was too much for him."

A moment of silence paused before Colonel Stone spoke again. "Arm yourself. Make sure Noel is armed too. Lord willing, the bat creatures will focus on the *Vanguard* and not even realize you guys are there."

"Ma'am," Farrell said, "I'm a pilot, not a soldier."

"Man up, Farrell," Colonel Stone roared at him. "You're a soldier now if you want to live. Get yourself armed and be ready if those things show up where you are. You and Noel are the only chance that the colonists in the *Seeder* have should McGregor and I fail."

"Yes, ma'am," Farrell responded weakly. "We'll do our best."

"And if we're not back in an hour, Farrell," Colonel Stone went on, "get Dropship Alpha back out into space and as far away from the planet as you can."

"You can count on that, Colonel," Farrell answered her.

"Stone, out," the colonel said and closed the channel, ending the transmission.

Farrell sat staring at the dropship's controls in front of him and feeling sick. Finally, he lurched from his seat and stumbled back to where Noel still sat on the dropship's floor near Brasiliat's corpse.

"He... He almost took me with him," Noel whimpered.

"He didn't though," Farrell said, trying to sound more together than he was. "Look, we need to get ourselves armed."

Farrell broke into one of the dropship's emergency caches and looked over at Noel. "You want a pistol or a rifle?"

Noel didn't respond.

Farrell selected a rifle from himself and grabbed a pistol for Noel. He moved over to where she sat and kneeled beside her, pressing the pistol into her hands.

"Take this," he ordered.

"Thank you," Noel said at last, nodding at him.

"And let's both pray to God that you won't need to use it," Farrell said, getting to his feet. "I need to get back up front. The colonel may need me."

"I'll go with you," Noel said and followed him into the pilot compartment, taking the copilot seat.

****

Dr. Lumley and Epiphany looked out of place as the small group made their way towards the *Vanguard*'s bridge. The shotgun the doctor carried seemed totally alien in his hands. It was Epiphany that bothered Colonel Stone though. The girl didn't seem to have any military discipline about her what-so-ever. Not even by the standards of the Fleet or Captain Merrick's often laid-back style of command, at times. The girl seemed just what she was: a *girl*. Colonel Stone placed Epiphany's age at around twenty. She had never met anyone like her. Despite the death and horror around them, Epiphany's eyes sparkled as if she were on a holiday and not a ship that was already a tomb to hundreds and likely to be their own too if they couldn't get the *Vanguard* out of the Talia system, and fast. Every gifted that Colonel Stone had met bore aspects in their personality that reflected the ability they possessed to some extent. This girl though, it was as if she knew no harm could possibly come to her. Charmed gifted were like the gifted known as *shields* in some ways. A shield gifted was an off-shoot of those with telekinesis whose gift basically called a telekinetic shield into existence about them when they were faced with danger. Colonel Stone had seen such shields, as they were called, bounce high-powered rounds away from themselves with no discernable effort. She'd even once seen a shield take a round from a tank and walk away from it to tell the story. With charmed though, it was similar but different. The charmed had no shields to protect them. Their gift was better described by saying that they had a guardian angel watching over them, one that always made sure they were never in harm's path to begin with. Being charmed went further than that though. A charmed gift would show up somewhere at the just the right time, duck at the right moment by bending over to fix their one their shoes, or the like. Colonel Stone hoped that having Epiphany with them would bring them luck too.

The four of them rode the lift to the bridge. McGregor stood at its door, ready for trouble. Dr. Lumley kept near the lift's rear, looking as terrified. Epiphany stood in the middle of the lift, humming a tune and tapping her foot to the music in her head. Colonel Stone was opposite McGregor's position, keeping her eyes fixed on the hatch-like door in the lift's top. With Brasiliat gone, the bat creatures could show up at any moment now, and there was no means of knowing where they would attack from when they did. Farrell had reported that hundreds of the creatures were already teleporting aboard the ship. So far, their group hadn't run into any of the things, but that would surely change. It was only a matter of time.

The doors of the lift swished apart, opening onto the bridge. McGregor leaped through the door, swinging his weapon about in an arc that swept the bridge. There were none of the bat creatures waiting on them there though. Colonel Stone was out of the lift next. She raced towards Captain Merrick's command chair. "McGregor, keep us covered!" she yelled. "Epiphany, take the helm."

"Me?" Epiphany giggled. "But I'm not a pilot."

"None of us are," Colonel Stone said. "Something tells me you're our best hope though."

"Okay, awesome." Epiphany nodded with a grin and practically danced her way over to the helm, sliding into its seat.

"Dr. Lumley," Colonel Stone gestured at the sensor console, "you're on sensors."

Looking relieved, Lumley headed over to the sensor station and propped his shotgun beside the seat he took there. Though the sensors of a starship weren't the same as the ones he used in medical, they were close enough that Colonel Stone believed he would be best at figuring them out and making them work.

"Run a full scan of the ship," Colonel Stone ordered. "I want to know how many bat creatures are already onboard and where they are at presently. If you happen to spot any other survivors, let me know at once."

"Will do." Lumley smiled, cracked his knuckles, and went to work at the task she had given him.

Captain Merrick's command chair had been built for a telemechanic. It was far from the standard one found on most ships like the *Vanguard*. Colonel Stone didn't have a prayer of using it effectively. As thus, instead of trying to use the chair to open a channel to Dropship Alpha in the hangar bay, she tapped her personal comm.

"Farrell," she said over the open channel. "We've reached the bridge. Stand by."

"Roger that," Farrell's voice answered her.

"Colonel!" Dr. Lumley called at her. "There are over two hundred of the bat creatures onboard if I am reading this right. They appear to be concentrated around the medical bay and engineering so far. I am picking up more teleporting in every few seconds though."

"Good job, Doctor." Colonel Stone nodded at Dr. Lumley.

"We need to get out of here," McGregor spoke up. "Even if we get the *Vanguard* out of the teleportation range of the creatures on the planet, it's already going to take something drastic to clear the ship of them again. The longer we wait, the worse it's going to get too."

"The man has a point," Dr. Lumley agreed. "If the creatures clustered outside of and in the engineering section start to go on a random rampage destroying whatever…"

"They could easily knock out a key system," Colonel Stone finished his thought. "Epiphany, does the helm have power?"

"Yep." The charmed grinned. "All the lights are green too. Pretty sure that's a good sign."

"Take us away from the planet," Colonel Stone ordered. "Maximum speed."

"I'll do my best." Epiphany smiled. The girl's fingers danced over the helm controls, flipping switches and powering up the ship's engines. The *Vanguard* almost seemed to moan as the great ship came about in space. Its engines came to life, launching it forward through space towards the edge of the Talia II system.

It was at that moment, when things went all pear-shaped. A bat creature appeared on the bridge between the helm station and the bridge's forward view screen. McGregor's shotgun thundered. Its blast caught the bat creature in its stomach, sending strands of intestines and splashes of black blood flying. The creature flopped over, rolling about on the floor of the bridge, as it tried to shove its guts back inside its body. McGregor quickly stepped closer to it and finished the bat creature with a second shot that blew its head apart in a shower of gore.

"Lumley!" Colonel Stone yelled as two more of the bat creatures suddenly appeared. One was dangerously close to where the doctor sat at the sensor station. Lumley heard her warning and grabbed for his weapon. The bat creature was ready for that though and slapped it from his hands. Dr. Lumley's face contorted in pain as a blade of bone burst from his forearm above his hand. Lumley threw himself forward, sinking the sword-like extension of bone into the bat creature's throat. It gurgled as black blood spewed from its mouth like vomit. Lumley jerked the blade free from the thing's throat and stabbed it again in the center of its chest. The bat creature died instantly as the bone blade pierced its heart.

The other bat creature that had appeared had lunged at McGregor. The former APC driver managed to get his shotgun into position in time to fire a point-blank shot into the thing. The shotgun's blast sent it reeling to topple over backwards. The bat creature lay there as a puddle of black bled out around its body, slicking the floor of the bridge. Colonel Stone could see the massive, ragged hole the shotgun had blown in its chest.

"We're clear of the planet, ma'am!" Epiphany shouted over the battle raging on the bridge as another half dozen bat creatures teleported onto it. "We should be clearing teleportation range in the next thirty seconds!"

"Lumley!" Colonel Stone shouted as she sprang out of the command chair, sweeping two of the bat creatures that had just appeared with a stream of fully automatic fire from her rifle. Their bodies jerked about as the rounds from her rifle dug into their flesh. "Get back on those sensors! We'll cover you!"

The blade of bone that had grown from his forearm had sunk back inside his body as Lumley dived into the sensor station's seat. One of the newly arrived bats took off into the air, soaring just below the bridge's ceiling towards him. Colonel Stone took careful aim and put a three-round burst into the side of the creature's head. Brain matter exited its skull alongside the bullets that plowed through it. The momentum of its flight carried its corpse on passed where Lumley sat to crash into the bridge's lift doors with the sound of snapping bones.

McGregor was busy fighting for his life with one of the bat creatures that managed to close in on him. Its clawed hands clutched his shotgun as it tried to wrestle the weapon out of his grasp. McGregor must have realized he couldn't win a contest of strength with the bat creature. He released his hold on the weapon, letting it go. The bat creature lost its balance from the sudden change as McGregor drew the pistol holstered on his hip and shot the creature between its eyes. Its head snapped back as the bullet dug a hole into and through its skull. McGregor put two more rounds into the creature as it fell to the floor. It didn't get up.

"Lumley!" Colonel Stone shouted again. "Are these guys coming from the ship or the planet?"

"No new lifeforms onboard!" Lumley shouted. "These are coming here from within the ship!"

That was it then. They had escaped. Now, they just had to survive long enough for the *Seeder* to reach the system. Knowing there would be no more of the things coming from the planet renewed Colonel Stone's determination to kick some bat creature arse. She brought the barrel of his rifle around to aim at a trio of bats clamoring towards her. She squeezed the trigger of her weapon, hosing them. Even as they fell, however, a fourth bat creature she hadn't noticed in time was suddenly behind her. Colonel Stone cried out as the claws of both its hands plunged into her back. The last thing she felt was her spinal column being ripped from her body before her corpse toppled face first to the bridge's floor.

****

Not a single one of the bat creatures had targeted Epiphany where she sat the helm until Colonel Stone had died. As the colonel's body hit the floor, Epiphany had jumped out of her seat and raced to the colonel's side. She had known the colonel was dead but had prayed it might not really be true until she saw the mangled mess of the colonel's back up close.

The bat creature that had killed Colonel Stone towered over her, shaking the colonel's spinal column in the air like some sort of victory rattle. Epiphany had no weapon of her own. She had misplaced it when she took the *Vanguard*'s helm. Colonel Stone's rifle was on the floor next to her though within easy reach. She snatched it up and leveled its barrel at the bat creature above her. Squeezing the weapon's trigger, she emptied what remained of its magazine into the bat creature's groin. The shriek of pain it gave as it died echoed on the bridge. Never had Epiphany heard such a high-pitched and horrid cry. She let go for the empty rifle, letting it clatter to the floor, to cover her ears with her hands.

"Epiphany! Look out!" Dr. Lumley screamed as he charged towards her. Epiphany saw Dr. Lumley hurl himself over her to tackle a bat creature that was approaching her from behind. The doctor and the bat thudded to the floor with Lumley on top. The bat creature's claws raked and slashed Dr. Lumley, tearing long groove over the flesh of his chest, arms, and stomach. Dr. Lumley didn't appear to feel any of it though. It was as if he had turned the pain receptors of his body off and likely he had done just that. Lumley opened his mouth and vomited concentrate stomach acid into the bat creature's face. The bat squealed and thrashed about beneath Lumley as the strange acid melted the hair from its body and its features into nothingness. Dr. Lumley shot her a sad look and then collapsed on top of the bat. The acid on it smoked and burnt at him where it touched his flesh, but Epiphany knew that Dr. Lumley was already dead. The actions he had taken to save her had cost him his life.

Only she and McGregor remained now, and they were currently outnumbered five to one. McGregor started to yell something at her but never got the chance. A bat, flying about the bridge in a fury, sliced his throat open from side to side with the razored edge of one of its wings. Blood erupted from McGregor's slit throat in a geyser of red.

Epiphany rose to her feet. She stood in the center of the bridge as the ten bat creatures circled about her. She had no weapon with which to fight them but nonetheless, she stared at them in pure defiance. As she had gotten up from the floor, her hand had brushed Colonel Stone's head. She found the colonel's comm. unit clinched in her fingers. She activated it and spoke directly into it as she raised it to her lips. "Farrell, get off the ship! Now!"

The bat creatures surged forward at her, all at the same time. Epiphany tried to dodge them, toppling into the ship's command chair, and then they were on her. Their claws cut into her, peeling her flesh from her bones in long stands. The teeth of some of the creatures sunk into her as she thrashed about. As her body twisted wildly about in the command chair, her flapping arms and kicking feet hit a series of its key in just the right order. An artificial voice boomed throughout the bridge.

"Please confirm self-destruct. Please confirm self-destruct," it urged her.

Spitting and choking on her own blood, Epiphany managed to squeal, "Self-destruct confirmed!"

Both she and the bat creatures eating and tearing at her were consumed in an explosion of fire and heat that swept over the bridge. Other explosions followed after it ripping their way throughout the *Vanguard.*

****

Farrell had received Epiphany's message and acted on it without even thinking about it. It was as if some strange force told him to believe her and kicked Dropship Alpha into gear. The dropship flew out of the *Vanguard*'s hangar as waves of fire that burst outward from the dying ship licked at its backside. Farrell kept the dropship's speed at maximum until it was well clear of the shrapnel-like bits of the *Vanguard* that broke apart and spun away from what remained of its burning hull into space.

"We're clear!" Farrell shouted in utter astonishment and relief.

Noel sat beside him in Dropship Alpha's copilot seat. Though she was physically next to him, Farrell could see that she was using her gift and her mind was actually far away. He didn't press her. He figured she would return her attention to her body and him when she was finished with whatever she was doing. Instead, he focused on using the last of Dropship Alpha's fuel to put a tad more distance between it and the planet of Talia II while also attempting to make sure the dropship would be within the *Seeder*'s path when the massive colony ship entered the system.

A minute or so later, Noel snapped upright in the copilot's seat. "You're right, Farrell. We're clear. We're out of the bats' range as far as I can tell, and none of the ones aboard the *Vanguard* as she blew had the time to locate us with their minds and attempt to blink aboard."

"I never thought I would be so happy just to be alive," Farrell said.

"We're not out of the woods yet though, are we?" Noel asked, as if she sensed the deeper thoughts he wasn't saying out loud.

Farrell's lips curled into a frown. "Yeah, I suppose we're not. All the maneuvering I've had to do used up our fuel. We're on reserve power," he admitted.

"So what does that mean?" Noel asked.

"It means if the *Seeder* doesn't show up soon, they're going to find us frozen to death like human popsicles in this dropship," Farrell said. "The heat will go long before we run out of air, water, or food."

"Could be worse I guess," Noel commented, trying to be strong.

"Yeah," Farrell said with a fake laugh. "I guess it could."

END

AUTHOR BIO

Eric S Brown is the author of numerous book series including the Bigfoot War series, the Kaiju Apocalypse series (with Jason Cordova), the Crypto-Squad series (with Jason Brannon), the Homeworld *Seeder* series (With Tony Faville and Jason Cordova), the Jack Bunny Bam series, and the A Pack of Wolves series. Some of his stand alone books include War of the Worlds plus Blood Guts and Zombies, Kraken, Taskforce, Alien Battalion, The Last Fleet, Sasquatch Lake, Kaiju Armageddon, Megalodon, Megalodons, and Megalodon Apocalypse to name only a few. His short fiction has been published hundreds of times in the small press in beyond including markets like the Onward Drake and Black Tide Rising anthologies from Baen Books, the Grantville Gazette, the SNAFU Military horror anthology series, and Walmart World magazine. He has done the novelizations for such films as Boggy Creek: The Legend is True (Studio 3 Entertainment) and The Bloody Rage of Bigfoot (Great Lake films). The first book of his Bigfoot War series was adapted into a feature film by Origin Releasing in 2014. Werewolf Massacre at Hell's Gate was the second his books to be adapted into film in 2015. In addition to his fiction, Eric also writes an award winning comic book news column entitled "Comics in a Flash." Eric lives in North Carolina with his wife and two children where he continues to write tales of the hungry dead, blazing guns, and the things that lurk in the woods.

CHECK OUT OTHER GREAT SCIENCE FICTION BOOKS

FURNACE
by Joseph Williams

On a routine escort mission to a human colony, Lieutenant Michael Chalmers is pulled out of hyper-sleep a month early. The RSA Rockne Hummel is well off course and—as the ship's navigator—it's up to him to figure out why. It's supposed to be a simple fix, but when he attempts to identify their position in the known universe, nothing registers on his scans. The vessel has catapulted beyond the reach of starlight by at least a hundred trillion light-years. Then a planetary-mass object materializes behind them. It's burning brightly even without a star to heat it. Hundreds of damaged ships are locked in its orbit. The crew discovers there are no life-signs aboard any of them. As system failures sweep through the Hummel, neither Chalmers nor the pilot can prevent the vessel from crashing into the surface near a mysterious ancient city. And that's where the real nightmare begins.

LUNA
by Rick Chesler

On the threshold of opening the moon to tourist excursions, a private space firm owned by a visionary billionaire takes a team of non-astronauts to the lunar surface. To address concerns that the moon's barren rock may not hold long-term allure for an uber-wealthy clientele, the company's charismatic owner reveals to the group the ultimate discovery: life on the moon.

But what is initially a triumphant and world-changing moment soon gives way to unrelenting terror as the team experiences firsthand that despite their technological prowess, the moon still holds many secrets.

CHECK OUT OTHER GREAT
SCIENCE FICTION BOOKS

IN PERPETUITY
by Jake Bible

For two thousand years, Earth and her many colonies across the galaxy have fought against the Estelian menace. Having faced overwhelming losses, the CSC has instituted the largest military draft ever, conscripting millions into the battle against the aliens. Major Bartram North has been tasked with the unenviable task of coordinating the military education of hundreds of thousands of recruits and turning them into troops ready to fight and die for the cause.

As Major North struggles to maintain a training pace that the CSC insists upon, he realizes something isn't right on the Perpetuity. But before he can investigate, the station dissolves into madness brought on by the physical booster known as pharma. Unfortunately for Major North, that is not the only nightmare he faces- an armada of Estelian warships is on the edge of the solar system and headed right for Earth!

BATTLEFIELD MARS
by David Robbins

Several centuries into the future, Earth has established three colonies on Mars. No indigenous life has been discovered, and humankind looks forward to making the Red Planet their own.

Then 'something' emerges out of a long-extinct volcano and doesn't like what the humans are doing.

Captain Archard Rahn, United Nations Interplanetary Corps, tries to stem the rising tide of slaughter. But the Martians are more than they seem, and it isn't long before Mars erupts in all-out war.

CHECK OUT OTHER GREAT SCIENCE FICTION BOOKS

MAUSOLEUM 2069
by **Rick Jones**

Political dignitaries including the President of the Federation gather for a ceremony onboard Mausoleum 2069. But when a cloud of interstellar dust passes through the galaxy and eclipses Earth, the tenants within the walls of Mausoleum 2069 are reborn and the undead begin to rise. As the struggle between life and death onboard the mausoleum develops, Eriq Wyman, a one-time member of a Special ops team called the Force Elite, is given the task to lead the President to the safety of Earth. But is Earth like Mausoleum 2069? A landscape of the living dead? Has the war of the Apocalypse finally begun? With so many questions there is only one certainty: in space there is nowhere to run and nowhere to hide.

RED CARBON
by **D.J. Goodman**

Diamonds have been discovered on Mars.

After years of neglect to space programs around the world, a ruthless corporation has made it to the Red Planet first, establishing their own mining operation with its own rules and laws, its own class system, and little oversight from Earth. Conditions are harsh, but its people have learned how to make the Martian colony home.

But something has gone catastrophically wrong on Earth. As the colony leaders try to cover it up, hacker Leah Hartnup is getting suspicious. Her boundless curiosity will lead her to a horrifying truth: they are cut off, possibly forever. There are no more supplies coming. There will be no more support. There is no more mission to accomplish. All that's left is one goal: survival.

www.ingramcontent.com/pod-product-compliance
Lightning Source LLC
Chambersburg PA
CBHW051958170626
46808CB00007B/2685